Two Thighs To Every Story

In Cold Bloom

Steve A. Anderson

Copyright © 2025 by Steve A. Anderson

ISBN: Softcover   978-0-9964781-9-9
ISBN: Hardcover 979-8-9995266-0-1
ISBN: eBook   979-8-9995266-1-8

Published by Steamboat Pubs

Printing in the United States of America

First Edition August 2025

Author's Note

This is a work of fiction. Names, characters, places, and incidents are products of the author's imagination or are used fictitiously. Any resemblance to actual people, living or dead, or actual events is purely coincidental.

Two Thighs To Every Story – In Cold Bloom is a sequel to the novel *Two Thighs To Every Story – Above Suspicion*. While this story can stand alone, readers may find deeper connections and richer context by reading the first book.

Contents

Prologue

Rooted Secrets

Shadow Bay had a silence to it.

Not the kind born of peace, but of knowing. A hush that clung to the trees and hung low over rooftops like fog that forgot how to lift. In spring, the town smelled of wet evergreens, thawed regret, and secrets too stubborn to rot.

People came to Shadow Bay to disappear. What they didn't realize was that ghosts traveled light.

Sydney Collins stood barefoot in her kitchen, tea steaming in one hand, her eyes fixed on the shadowed trail vanishing behind her home. Pine needles slick with rain stitched a path into the woods. Somewhere down that trail lay choices she could never take back.

Behind her, a malpractice complaint from the Oregon Medical Review Board sat on the kitchen table, white and thin, accusing. She hadn't touched it since yesterday.

Instead, her gaze slid once again to the corner of the living room, where the old secretary desk sat like a courtroom witness too loyal to break. The bottom drawer, still slightly crooked from the move, never closed right. Ryan and Spencer had nicked it, hauling it in, and patched it with glue and marker, but it never fully held. Neither did the truth.

Inside that drawer was the journal. The one she began after John's funeral. The one she never reread. It held entries written in her own hand, precise, measured, and damning. Mentions of the oleander tea with regrets dressed as rationale.

She used to believe in rules. Boundaries. Ethics. But ethics didn't raise a son. And some marriages don't end in death; they end in decisions.

Bill had only suggested the oleander plant. It was Sydney who made the cocktail for John.

Ryan would be home soon, just a few weeks away from finishing Stanford Medical School, with his hematology residency lined up, and a bright future ahead. He was the kind of son people dreamed about, and the kind Sydney had nearly destroyed herself to protect.

And now, letters from a Texas law firm hinted that Dalton's estate had unfinished business. Dalton, the man who knew Ryan's DNA better than any living soul.

Then there was David. Brilliant. Helpful. Too helpful. His questions about the clinic's AI implementation, the finances, and the expansion, along with his polished curiosity, left her uneasy.

Secrets have a half-life. And Sydney was beginning to feel the radiation burn.

She walked to the secretary desk, knelt beside the drawer, and pressed her palm against it, not to open it, just to feel its refusal.

It held.

For now.

Rising, she took her tea to the back porch and left the malpractice complaint on the table.

Outside, the fog thickened around the trees like breath on a mirror. Somewhere beneath

Raincrest Cellars' vineyard soil and grape vine roots, things were beginning to stir.

In Shadow Bay, some secrets are buried. Others are pruned. But all of them bloom eventually.

The Main Characters

Sydney Collins - Medical Nurse Practitioner

Dr. Ryan Collins – Hematology - Sydney's Son

Bill Collins – Sydney's father-in-law & Ryan's Grampa

David Smith – Software Developer – Artificial Intelligence

Valerie Cavanaugh – Vineyard Owner

Sheriff Howard Truman – Lane County Sheriff

Part I

Shifting Ground

Chapter 1 - Settling Ashes

The spring air in Shadow Bay still carried a damp chill in the mornings, but Sydney preferred it that way. It reminded her of the space between seasons, neither cold nor warm, just unsettled, like her.

As she stood at the edge of her garden, reflecting on how Ryan and Spencer, before the crash, had struggled with her heirloom secretary. The damaged corner had been more than just a scratch in the wood; it had been a crack in the facade of her carefully constructed life.

She hadn't known then that Spencer would find the diary.

Hadn't known he'd read the words she'd scrawled amongst her depression and desperation: *"John's tea. Oleander. No more questions."*

Now, Spencer was gone. Dalton was gone. And the only people left who knew the truth were her, Bill... and the earth itself, which had a way of unearthing what was buried.

A gust of wind shook the oleander plant, now taking root in the garden. The same plant that Bill had given her. The same one that had ended two lives.

Sydney exhaled. Some poisons didn't just kill. They lingered.

Dalton's name no longer came up in local conversation, not since the plane crash had become old news and the story had faded into the background of local gossip. John's name never came up much anymore, either. But for Sydney, the silence echoed louder than words. Her secret still filled the spaces of what-ifs, the way grief does when it chooses not to leave.

Staring past the daffodils and early irises in her garden, the oleander plant, now more like a bush, was bursting with pink petals, looking deceptively innocent. A poisonous beauty, like so many truths she had learned to live with.

The medical clinic was no longer just a rural outpost for basic care. It was becoming something more, a regional hub with modern diagnostics and specialty medicine, yet still rooted in compassionate care.

Dr. Bell, the clinic's original neurologist and a quiet, brilliant force, had partnered with Sydney from the beginning. She treated migraines, seizures, traumatic brain injuries, and aging patients grappling with memory loss. Sydney's caseload focused on chronic conditions, primarily diabetes, obesity, and arthritis. She'd become a trusted presence in town, not just as a nurse practitioner but a clinic partner. And now, with Ryan set to graduate with a specialty in hematology, she would soon welcome her son as a partner in the clinic.

The Shadow Bay Medical Clinic had always been a quiet cornerstone of the town, a place where Dr. Bell's neurological expertise steadied aging hands and traumatized minds, while Sydney's pragmatic care managed the slow creep of obesity, diabetes, and arthritis. Their partnership had thrived on contrast: Bell's razor-sharp diagnostics paired with Sydney's instinct for patient trust. But now, with Ryan's impending return as a hematologist, the clinic was on the verge of something bigger. *Expansion.*

The blueprints sprawled across Sydney's desk showed an added modernized wing, its design punctuated by AI integration, automated patient triage, predictive analytics for chronic disease management, and even a prototype algorithm to cross-reference symptoms with rare blood disorders, Ryan's specialty. They even started sketching long-range plans for a joint clinic venture with orthopedic specialists, focused on minimally invasive spine and knee procedures. The town didn't know it yet, but Shadow Bay was about to outgrow its "remote and rural" status.

David had been a quiet constant in Sydney's life since meeting him shortly after moving into her new home. He showed a steady presence who'd shown up at the clinic with a donation for Ryan's Acute Myeloid Leukemia (AML) fund, then stayed close to help her navigate the new AI software that no one else really understood yet. David had been just a tech consultant with a knack for simplifying new computer updates and the chaos they initially presented. Now, as his fingers brushed hers over the clinic's new AI schematics, she caught the shift in his smile. Warmer. *Intentional.*

"You've got the best hands-on approach in the Valley," he said, tapping the blueprint where her expansion plans would double their clinic suites.

"But even you can't predict every variable. Let my AI systems handle the patterns. You handle the people."

The compliment was butter-smooth, but Sydney felt the hook beneath it. David had always been generous with praise and light on personal details. She knew he'd grown up in Portland, that his first startup had failed, and that he hated cilantro. She didn't know why he'd really moved to Shadow Bay, or how he'd known to ask about John's old insurance policies last year.

She laughed, pulling her hand back to adjust the collar of her lab coat.

"Flattery won't get you a discount on medical fees."

"Wouldn't dream of it." He leaned against her desk, close enough that she caught the cedar scent of his cologne.

"But dinner might. Tomorrow? That new place on the lake?"

Sydney hesitated. A couple of months ago, before the expansion plans, she'd have said yes without thinking. Now, her pause stretched just a beat too long, long enough to notice how David's gaze flicked to the framed photo of Ryan on her shelf. Studying it? Or just being polite?

"Let's see how the budget meeting goes," she deflected, turning back to the blueprints.

Sydney had met with David and liked the potential but insisted on safeguards. No full access to patient histories. No unvetted data streams. She'd seen how algorithms could hurt as easily as they could heal.

Still, the proposed upgrades were undeniable. The new hematology lab would allow Ryan to run advanced genomic testing locally, sparing patients the three-hour drive to Portland. Dr. Bell, though wary of machines replacing intuition, had conceded to AI-assisted brain mapping for her dementia cases.

"As long as it's a tool, not a crutch," she'd muttered.

A silent partner, Sydney's father-in-law Bill, had helped fund the new wing, quietly, discreetly, but with deep pockets and a watchful eye. His investment bought them the new imaging suite, and the AI diagnostic software David had mentioned could soon be layered into it, if Sydney could trust him. She'd run a deeper background check on him. Just in case.

Just as construction crews were being finalized to break ground, Sydney noticed something unsettling: David had taken an unusual interest in the clinic's archived medical records. Then came a late-night glitch in the AI system's security logs, barely a blip, but enough to reveal that

John's old file had been accessed. She tried to dismiss it. A coincidence, perhaps. But a gnawing question lingered: had the algorithm already traced the toxic thread back to her? Had it uncovered the poison she thought was buried in her past for good?

Chapter 2 - The Heir

Sydney's phone buzzed.

Ryan: "Can't believe it's this Saturday."

She swallowed her anxiety and typed back:

"I'm proud of you. Can't wait to celebrate."

Later that week, she and Bill would fly to Palo Alto for Ryan's graduation from Stanford.

The California sun cast its golden glow over the Stanford campus, filtering through redwoods that stood like sentinels of tradition and ambition. Sydney adjusted the lapel of her soft linen blazer as the crowd of families and graduates slowly found their seats. Bill stood beside her, proud as ever, donning a new tie that clashed just enough with his shirt to let everyone know it was a special day.

The Stanford Medical School commencement ceremony unfolded with elegance and precision. A string quartet played softly behind the stage. When Ryan's name was called, Sydney's breath caught in her throat. There he was, her son, walking across the stage in his crimson robe and doctoral hood, tall and composed, a Stanford-trained physician specializing in hematology. She saw a flicker of Dalton in the way he held his jaw, the quiet confidence in his stride, though Ryan would never know the full measure of what he'd inherited.

A few feet from her, Bill wiped his eye with a monogrammed handkerchief, playing it off as a reaction to the spring pollen.

Later that evening, the four of them sat at an upscale Mediterranean restaurant near Palo Alto, celebrating over grilled salmon and toasting with a glass of Pinot Noir. Arielle, seated beside Ryan, was all charm, polished and warm, but just a touch too polished for Sydney's liking. There was something in the way she steered conversations, always returning to Ryan's future or mentioning her job at the biotech startup, always brushing her hand against Ryan's as if claiming territory.

Sydney smiled politely and offered nothing more than cordial approval, but inside, her instincts stirred. She'd learned to listen to them, especially after John. Sometimes it was the small tells, the gaps between sentences, or how someone asked a question that told you more than the answer.

After dessert, they returned to the hotel lounge where Sydney finally turned to Ryan, her glass of prosecco still half full.

"You've done something extraordinary, Ryan," she said. "And it's time we made a place for you where you belong, on your terms."

Bill leaned forward, his elbows resting on the table. "We've been talking," he said.

"Shadow Bay's medical clinic is expanding. Neurology, diabetes, and now... hematology. We want you as a partner, not just staff. Build something of your own, with us."

Ryan looked stunned for a moment, then softened, eyes shining not just from wine or pride, but something deeper, belonging, purpose.

"That means more than you know," he said. "I want that. I really do." Laughing in disbelief. "You really think Shadow Bay is ready for bone marrow panels and iron panels on the same street as the bait shop?"

Sydney raised a brow. "Ready or not. It's coming."

Arielle smiled, too brightly. "That's amazing, babe. Oregon's beautiful. I've always said I could work remotely for a while..."

Sydney's polite nod didn't mask the chill she felt inside.

Two Weeks Later – Shadow Bay

Ryan's boxes were still half-unpacked in the guest room of Sydney's log home, sunlight stretching across the wood floor in a soft grid. The hummingbirds buzzed at the feeder outside as Ryan adjusted to the quiet hum of the bay and the long trails he'd begun running in the mornings. It was different than Palo Alto, slower, cleaner, a bit mysterious, but he was once again warming up to it. He liked it.

A knock came just before 8 am. Sydney, in her scrubs, peeked out the window. A FedEx truck idled near the drive.

"Ryan? For you," she called, walking back inside with a flat white envelope.

He took it from her, brow furrowing at the return address: Whitaker & Lang, Probate Attorneys – Dallas, Texas.

Opening the envelope, he pulled out a heavy set of documents. The cover letter was formal, bearing a probate court seal. The words "surviving descendant" and "Dr. Dalton Avery Estate" leapt out at him like sudden thunder.

He read on, jaw tightening.

"They're... trying to reach me. Something about Dalton's estate and will."

Sydney's expression froze as she took in the seal and Dalton's name. Her chest tightened. So many buried things had begun to rise again.

Inside was a formal letter and supporting documents. Ryan read it twice before sitting down on the garden bench.

As the sole surviving biological kin to the late Dr. Dalton Avery, Ryan N. Collins may have legal standing as a beneficiary in the absence of an updated will. However, said estate is now being contested by Ms. Caroline Bade, niece of the late Ms. Abigail Avery (deceased spouse of Dr. Dalton Avery). Ms. Bade asserts her aunt acted in anti-lapse and is filing to claim a share of the estate as next of kin and domestic heir." In the absence of an updated testamentary document, the estate fell under the jurisdiction of intestate succession laws, subject to interpretation under the Texas probate code.

Ms. Caroline Bade, the niece of Dalton's deceased wife, claim rests on the fact that Dalton's will named his late wife as the sole beneficiary. Since the wife predeceased him and there was no codicil or subsequent amendment, Caroline asserts that she, as the closest living relative of Dalton's spouse, holds a rightful interest, arguing that the estate should revert to the wife's kin under a doctrine known as "anti-lapse" (designed to keep assets within a familial line if the named beneficiary dies before the testator).

Sydney glanced over at Ryan and closed her eyes. She had known this day would come, just not now, not like this. Dalton's will hadn't been updated after he reconnected with Ryan, and with both Dalton and Spencer gone, Ryan's claim wasn't as clean as it should've been. Ryan legally remained Dalton's unrecognized son.

Sydney knew Dalton's estate would follow them home, as legal messes never respected timing.

Ryan was home now, and her clinic was growing.

Sydney smiled at Ryan as their eyes met, "We'll discuss this legal fight another day."

But the past? The past was still breathing, and now with lawyers. But Dalton's Estate was certainly worth a legal fight.

Chapter 3 – Shadows Among the Vines

The tasting barn at Raincrest Cellars was buzzing, its high-beamed ceiling echoing with laughter, clinking glasses, and the warm rustle of familiar conversation. The Willamette Valley Winegrowers' Cooperative held its quarterly meeting like clockwork, part business, part celebration. For some, it was about harvest yields, reports, and distributor headaches. For Bill, it was about something more.

He'd developed a quiet obsession with wine, in particular, Pinot Noir, ever since his semi-retirement began, not just drinking it but *understanding* it. Soil types, clone selection, and fermentation variables. It was a puzzle that made sense of his restless mind. But tonight, something besides wine caught his attention.

She stood alone at the back table near the food spread, a slender woman with silver-threaded dark hair pulled loosely over one shoulder. She poured a taste of her 2022 estate Pinot with calm grace and the quiet detachment of someone who'd once loved this world deeply but now stood slightly apart from it.

"Evening," Bill said, lifting a glass in polite greeting.

"I hear this is the wine that made the Raincrest Cellars local competition cry."

Her mouth lifted in a weary smile. "He said 'weep,' actually. I think he had a cold. But I'll take it."

"Valerie Cavanaugh?" he asked, offering his hand.

"Yes."

"I'm Bill Collins. I've been nosing around vineyards lately. May be looking to partner or invest. Heard yours had soul."

She nodded cautiously. "It used to. Maybe it still does. Depends on the day."

They talked. Not about yields or frost protection or rootstock, but about legacy, and loss, and how grief seeps into the barrels if you're not careful.

Valerie swirled her glass of Pinot, the garnet liquid catching the late afternoon light filtering through the tasting room's cedar beams. "Twenty years next spring," she said, her voice softening.

"Mark was only forty-eight when the doctors told him his heart wasn't built for the skies anymore. A pilot's life, always up there, never rooted." She gestured toward the rolling rows of vines beyond the windows, their leaves gilded by the sun.

"But this place? He called it his 'crash landing.' Said the earth here had a pulse he could finally sync up with."

Bill followed her gaze to the slope where the first Pinot Noir blocks had been planted, now gnarled and wise with age. Valerie's laugh was bittersweet.

"We bought this land outside Shadow Bay on a whim. Just an overgrown orchard then. The Red Hills soil was stubborn, but Mark swore it'd grow something extraordinary. He'd kneel in the dirt at dawn, checking each vine like it was a flight plan." Her fingers tightened around the stem of her glass.

"I handled the people, the tastings, the wine club dinners, and also helped with the final stages of the wine itself. He hated crowds in the cockpit, but here? He'd linger with guests until last call, telling stories about the '12 vintage like it was a cockpit legend."

A shadow crossed her face as she glanced toward the stone cellar, its arched door slightly ajar. "This land was his second chance. He said flying took him away from people. The wine? She paused, her smile fading, that brought them back."

The unspoken words hung heavy between them *until they didn't.* Until the cellar steps, the unnatural angle of his body, the coroner's quiet doubt. Valerie drained her glass, the silence louder than the hum of the cooling tanks downstairs.

She admitted she kept the vineyard going partly for routine, partly for stubbornness, and partly because she didn't know who she was without it.

And Bill didn't push. He didn't ask for financials or parcel maps. Instead, he simply said,

"Would you ever consider a partnership? Someone to walk the rows with, not just run the books?"

Taco Thursday at Sydney's Home

Sydney's house smelled like lime, cilantro, and blistered tortillas. Her open-plan kitchen was bustling with energy as bowls of shredded pork, fire-roasted salsa, and crumbled queso fresco made their rounds across the butcher-block island. *Taco Thursdays* were a monthly family tradition, part therapy and part reunion.

Ryan leaned against the counter, sipping a sparkling lime water, teasing Sydney about her overzealous spice level.

When Bill arrived, he wasn't alone.

"This," he said, placing two bottles of red on the table and gesturing to his guest, "is Valerie Cavanaugh. She makes the wine that made the other area vineyards cry."

Sydney looked up from her cutting board, wiping her hands on a towel, curiosity already lighting in her eyes.

"I've heard of Raincrest Cellars. Welcome. I'm Sydney."

Valerie smiled politely but held herself tight. Bill could see it, the guarded politeness, the social muscle memory. She was used to fending for herself, even when among friendly faces.

"This is my son, Dr. Ryan Collins," Sydney said.

Ryan stepped forward with that ease that made people feel seen.

"Nice to meet you. Pinot or Chardonnay?"

Valerie grinned faintly. "Both, but I'm told my Pinot has more bite."

"Good," Ryan replied. "So does my mother."

They laughed, and something loosened. Over tacos and casual chatter, Valerie began to thaw. She spoke about vineyard rituals, soil temperature obsessions, and the lonely rhythm of tending land that had once belonged to two hearts.

Bill Pays a Visit to Raincrest Cellars

The morning fog clung to the rolling hills of Willamette Valley as Bill pulled up to the Raincrest Cellars vineyard, the rows of Pinot Noir and Chardonnay vines stretching out in perfect symmetry. Valerie was already waiting near the ATV, her sleeves rolled up and her boots dusted with soil. She gave him a quick smile, warm but businesslike.

"Ready for the grand tour?" she asked, tossing him a spare pair of work gloves.

Bill caught them, grinning. "Lead the way."

They set off through the vines, Valerie pointing out the different blocks, some newly planted, others decades old. She explained the meticulous work behind each stage: winter pruning, shoot thinning, the nerve-wracking dance of frost protection in spring. Bill listened intently, surprised by how much labor went into each bottle of wine.

Meeting the Crew

As they rode on, near the edge of the property, a group of workers moved methodically down the rows, their hands quick and practiced as they tied back vines. Valerie waved them over.

"This is Cesar," she said, nodding toward the foreman, a lean man with sharp eyes and a firm handshake.

"He's been with us for years. Knows these vines better than I do."

Cesar gave a curt nod. "Señor."

Bill shook his hand, catching the guarded edge in the man's tone. There was something there, not quite hostility, but caution. Valerie's gaze flickered between them, and Bill wondered if this was the suspicion she'd mentioned.

The rest of the crew greeted him politely, but he noticed how their eyes darted to Cesar before speaking. One younger worker, maybe late teens, hesitated before shaking Bill's hand, his grip too quick, his smile uneasy.

The Winemaking Side of Things

Pulling the ATV up to the barn, Valerie led Bill into the barrel room, where the damp, earthy scent of oak and fermenting wine filled the air. Stainless steel tanks gleamed under the low lights, and rows of barrels stood like silent sentinels, each holding the promise of next year's vintage.

"This is where the magic happens, or where we pray it does," Valerie said, running a hand along one of the barrels.

"Harvest is just the beginning. After the grapes come in, it's all about fermentation, pressing, and aging. One wrong move — too much oxygen, a bad yeast strain, and an entire lot's ruined."

Bill watched as she checked the bungs on a few barrels, her movements precise. "You handle all this yourself?"

She shook her head. "I've got a consulting winemaker who comes in during critical phases, but day-to-day, it's just me now and Hector, one of our cellar hands. He used to work at a big Sonoma winery before coming up here." She smirked.

"Though half the time, I think he humors me by pretending my guesses are as good as his experience."

The Face of the Winery: Tastings and Events

Back up to the tasting room, a small but charming space with a view of the valley, a woman with warm brown eyes and a no-nonsense ponytail was setting glasses on the bar.

"That's Luisa," Valerie said. Cesar's wife. She helps me with the tasting room when she's not chasing after their three kids."

Luisa looked up and smiled as they entered. "Ah, you brought a new investor," she teased, pouring a splash of chardonnay into a glass and sliding it toward Bill.

"Try this. Valerie says it's too dry, but the customers love it."

Valerie rolled her eyes but didn't argue. Instead, she gestured to the event calendar on the wall, packed with weekend tastings, weddings, and a fall harvest dinner.

"Luisa also handles most of the bookings. She has a way with people, gets the Portland wine snobs to actually relax and the bachelorette parties to behave."

Bill took a sip, surprised by the wine's bright, crisp finish. "You're good at this."

Luisa shrugged. "It's just talking and remembering that people don't buy wine, they buy the story." She shot a pointed look at Valerie. "Which is why someone needs to spend less time in the cellar and start schmoozing."

Valerie groaned. "I schmooze."

"You lecture, Luisa corrected. "There's a difference."

Bill laughed, but his attention snagged on the way Valerie's shoulders relaxed here, in this space. The vineyard was her obsession, but the winery? That was a living, breathing thing, a mix of science, luck, and the people who made it all hum.

And if Bill intended to be part of it, he'd need to learn both.

A Partnership in the Making?

Back at the ATV, Valerie wiped her hands on her jeans. "So, what do you think?"

Bill exhaled, looking out over the land. "It's a hell of a lot more work than I realized."

The vineyard looked idyllic in the evening light, rows of Pinot vines glowing amber against the soft rise of the hills. But Valerie wasn't fooled by the scenery, and she didn't pretend otherwise.

She laughed. "Yeah, and that's before hail, drought, or a bad frost wipes out half your crop."

He studied her, the way she talked about the vineyard, the pride in her voice despite the exhaustion lining her face. There was something magnetic about her determination.

Bill's eyes scanned the vineyard. "Have you given any more thought about bringing someone in, Val? Not just for the labor, but as a real partner."

Valerie raised an eyebrow. "Depends on the partner."

She stood with her arms crossed near the fermentation shed, wind tugging at a loose strand of hair.

"I won't lie, Bill, this place takes more than love for the land. It takes stamina, patience, and thick skin for supplier drama and broken bottling lines. And lately, it's been more stress than satisfaction." She turned toward him, her expression earnest.

"But I'm not ready to let go. Not yet. I believe Raincrest Cellars still makes the best wine in the valley, but I can't keep doing it alone. Not with César sniffing around like he owns a stake in it, and the rest of the crew now answering to him more than me."

Bill listened, taking in the weary edge to her voice, not defeat, but fatigue. She let out a breath and continued.

"So, here's what I'm thinking. Before either of us talk about shares or contracts, why don't you work alongside me? One full month, vineyard, cellar, tasting room, all of it. You'll get to know the place, the people, and whether it's something you want to be part of, really part of. Because the risks are real, Bill. But if this works... the reward isn't just profit. It's a legacy. And maybe a little peace of mind for both of us."

Before he could respond, a truck rumbled down the access road, kicking up dust. A man in sunglasses leaned out, saying something in rapid Spanish to Cesar before driving off. Valerie's jaw tightened.

"Friend of yours?" Bill asked lightly.

Valerie hesitated. "Just a supplier." But the way she said it told him otherwise.

Later, as they walked back to the main barn, she finally admitted it.

"There's... something going on. Money missing. Supplies disappearing. I think Cesar's involved, but I can't prove it."

Bill frowned. "You think it's theft?"

"Or worse." She lowered her voice.

"I've heard rumors about crews moving more than just grapes at night. If that's true, and the wrong people find out you're sniffing around..."

Bill met her eyes. "Then I guess we'd better find out fast."

She held his gaze, and for the first time, he saw something beyond the tough exterior, vulnerability, maybe even trust.

"Mark didn't just fall," she said softly. "That's what they all said. But I knew the way he moved around this place. He never would've missed that last step. He wasn't drunk. He wasn't careless."

Bill didn't speak, just waited.

"There were things he'd started noticing," she continued.

"About the workers. Not all of them. But César... he started asking questions about our property deed. About inheritance clauses. Then Mark was gone. Just gone."

She looked at Bill with haunted eyes.

"And now I get whispers. Suggestions. That I should sell... or give over shares. Like Mark had made promises I never heard about."

Bill's jaw tightened. "And you think someone's trying to push you out, too?"

"I don't know," she said, voice breaking. "I don't know what's grief and what's real anymore."

He reached for her hand and gripped it gently.

"Then let's find out."

And then, just like that, she smirked.

"You sure you still want in on this?"

Bill grinned back.

"You might change your mind after 30 days."

Part II

Cracks in the Soil

Chapter 4 – Courting Malpractice

The medical clinic buzzed like any other Thursday, phones chirping, keyboards clacking, and Sydney's shoes scuffing softly across the tile as she moved between exam rooms. Room 3 had a diabetic check-in; Room 5, a wellness consultation. She was midway through explaining insulin titration to a newly diagnosed teenager and his mother when a sharp knock interrupted the rhythm.

Without waiting for an answer, the door eased open. Kennedy, the front desk nurse, stood there awkwardly with a clipboard and a pale face. Behind her loomed a man in a windbreaker, his badge flashing with indifferent authority.

"Sydney Collins?" he asked, already knowing the answer.

Sydney's pulse kicked up. "Yes?"

"You've officially been served," he said sharply, thrusting the white envelope forward like a stinger.

The room was still. The mother blinked. The teenager's eyes darted between the man and Sydney like he was watching a courtroom drama unfold in real time.

"Please excuse me," Sydney said evenly, her hand tightening on the envelope as she took it.

"Lisa, can you finish this consult for me?"

She stepped out before the tremor in her voice could follow.

The clinic hallway stretched like a tunnel. Sydney didn't stop walking until she reached the private call room near the back of the building. She shut the door, dropped the envelope on the table, and stared at it as if it might detonate.

Inside was a malpractice complaint stamped clearly with the case number in the upper-right corner, filed in Lane County District Court.

When she finally peeled it open, her eyes went straight to the plaintiff's name: *Melanie Binder.*

It didn't register at first. Then it did.

Tall, tan, that flexible blonde who used to come in every few months complaining of joint pain and vague fatigue. She'd refused counseling, declined a specialist referral, and once stormed out when Sydney mentioned connective tissue disease.

Sydney flipped pages. Words hit like blows. *Failure to diagnose... emotional distress... irreversible vascular trauma... lifetime disability...*

Her stomach coiled. The suit painted her as reckless, cold, and dismissive, as if she'd willfully ignored a patient in need.

Bullshit. She pulled out her phone and called Bill.

By the time he arrived an hour later, Sydney had already rescheduled half her afternoon. She sat in her office with the blinds drawn, the complaint splayed across her desk like an autopsy.

Bill didn't speak at first. He just poured coffee into the chipped mug he kept here, the one with the faded Coast Guard emblem. Then he sat down across from her.

"Tell me."

Sydney exhaled. "She's claiming I missed a diagnosis of Ehlers-Danlos. That her aorta tore, and it could've been prevented."

Bill tilted his head. "Did you miss it?"

"She refused genetic testing. She didn't disclose family history. I tried, she pushed back. I offered a referral to Dr. Bell. She no-showed. We documented all of it."

He nodded. "Then this isn't malpractice. It's regret. Or maybe greed."

Sydney's voice cracked. "Still goes to court. Still goes in the papers. Still makes people question whether I know what I'm doing."

Bill leaned forward. "Let them question. We'll show them."

That night, Sydney sat alone in her log home in Shadow Bay, the lawsuit spread across the kitchen island beside a half-glass of wine she'd forgotten to drink. The lake outside was still, a mirror of the rising storm in her gut. She opened her laptop, pulled up Melanie's file, and started re-reading every clinical note. Every missed appointment. Every declining signature, before turning in. She barely slept.

By dawn, she was back at the kitchen table, the sharp black text of the complaint glaring under the pale light of morning.

"Complaint for Medical Negligence," the words pressed down on her like a boulder. It didn't matter that she had reviewed Melanie's labs thoroughly or that the clinic's charting protocols had been followed. Perception had become a liability. And now the process wouldn't wait for her to catch her breath.

Her laptop buzzed, a reminder for the Zoom call Ryan had insisted on before she left for the clinic. Sydney clicked *Join*.

Ryan's face filled the screen, worry instantly etched in his facial features. "I read the complaint, Mom."

"I know," she said quietly. "I'm calling Harbor Point after this."

The call, meant to be brief, stretched into a strategy session. As soon as Sydney shared her screen and walked him through the complaint, Ryan's usual relaxed expression faded. "This is serious," he said, leaning forward. "They're throwing around systemic negligence. If this goes to trial, it won't just be about one missed diagnosis. They'll come after your clinic's entire model."

Sydney exhaled. "She's not just coming after me. She's coming after small-town medicine. The rural clinic. Limited resources. It'll be painted as outdated. Unsafe."

Ryan squinted at the screen. "What does the chart say about Marfan or vEDS screening?"

"I flagged hypermobility on the second visit and recommended neurology follow-up. She declined."

"Signed refusals?"

"Twice," she said, pulling up the PDFs.

Ryan nodded. "Then we have a foundation. But you'll need more than paper. You'll need someone to interpret your decision-making. I can draft a hematologic risk summary... maybe even testify, if it goes that far."

A beat passed. "Also... have you told David yet?"

Sydney blinked. "Not yet."

Ryan's mouth tightened slightly. "He might want to know. Especially if you need to access anything in the Electronic Health Record (EHR) system."

Sydney gave a faint nod but didn't answer. The hesitation hung between them.

After the call ended, she sat in silence for a long moment, staring out at the lake. Then she reached for her phone. It was just past eight.

She scrolled through her contacts and found the number for Harbor Point Indemnity, her malpractice insurer for nearly a decade, but until now, only a line of fine print on a renewal notice.

The voice that answered was polite, professional, and disturbingly efficient. Sydney's own voice felt thin as she recited the case number and the date she'd been served, trying not to sound defensive or rattled. But each question made her stomach tighten:

"Was a formal complaint made to the clinic administrator?" "Do you have supporting documentation regarding informed consent?"

She hated this part, not the questions, but how they reduced years of careful medicine to a checklist of risk exposure. When the call ended, the only sound in the house was the hum of the refrigerator.

Harbor Point would assign legal counsel, they said. They would *handle it from here.* Still, the weight of the process now in motion felt very much her own.

She wasn't going to settle. Not without a fight. If Melanie wanted a trial, she'd get one.

But she wouldn't like the story Sydney was going to tell.

She grabbed her bag and headed out the door, the weight of the morning still pressing on her ribs. On the short drive to the clinic, she called David to let him know about the complaint, unaware that Ryan had already reached out to him for input.

That evening, David arrived with Thai and his usual easy confidence. His hair was still damp from a run, and his laptop bag slung over one shoulder like it was part of his anatomy.

"I heard from Ryan earlier today as well," he said, skipping the usual greeting. "I pulled your clinic's backend logs as soon as he called. You should see this."

He slid onto the stool across from Sydney and opened his laptop. With a few clicks, he brought up an interface far slicker than anything Sydney used at work. His AI platform, *VitalMind*, hummed beneath the hood, an evolving diagnostic tool he'd been quietly testing in rural clinics with Sydney's cautious blessing.

David tapped the screen. "Melanie's EHR shows refusal of referrals. But what's interesting is this metadata from the scheduling module. She rescheduled three times after being flagged for vascular risk. *VitalMind's* behavioral tracker tagged her as a *"risk minimizer,"* a pattern we've seen in patients who dodge difficult truths."

Sydney leaned in, stunned. "You're saying the AI predicted she was likely to reject serious findings?"

He nodded. "It's not admissible, yet. But it's persuasive."

He scrolled again. "Also, her digital footprint is strange. She accessed her patient portal last month six times. Specifically, the visit notes from last year."

Sydney raised a brow. "Before filing the lawsuit."

"Exactly."

David looked up. "If you want me on this, I can build a narrative from the data. Show that you followed protocol and that she was already curating her legal angle before you were even served."

Sydney's fingers tightened around her glass. "Build it."

She didn't say it out loud, but the thought flickered. If David could track this much digital detail on Melanie... What else could he trace?

Chapter 5 – The Will and the Way

Ryan parked his car in front of the modest brick building; the discreet brass sign etched with *Graham & Associates – Attorneys at Law* caught the pale morning sunlight. He sat for a moment, the engine ticking as it cooled, the estate letter in his inside jacket pocket suddenly feeling like it weighed a pound. Somewhere in the distance, a siren pierced the calm, then faded.

Inside, the receptionist greeted him quietly and led him down a carpeted hallway that muffled every step.

"Mr. Graham will see you now, Dr. Ryan," she said softly, opening a heavy oak door.

The lawyer's office exuded a quiet authority. Oak-paneled walls, floor-to-ceiling shelves of leather-bound casebooks, and a diploma from Northwestern lent it both gravity and a subtle warning: this is where serious matters are resolved.

Mr. Graham stood to greet him. Mid-sixties, silver hair brushed neatly to the side, his handshake was firm but not aggressive, like a man who'd long ago learned that persuasion beats intimidation.

"Dr. Ryan, it's good to meet you. Have a seat," he said, gesturing to a leather chair that looked older than Ryan.

"Thanks," Ryan replied, sitting down. He declined the offer of coffee or water with a small shake of the head.

Mr. Graham got right to it.

"I've reviewed the file you sent and the early court notices. As you probably gathered, Dalton's niece, Caroline, is contesting the will."

"She claims I don't belong in it at all," Ryan said, voice tight.

"That Dalton never formally acknowledged me."

"Well," Graham said, steepling his fingers, "this case is more about what the law sees than what it feels. Caroline's objection focuses on the lack of an updated will, which is accurate; Dalton never amended it after learning about you. But here's where it gets interesting: you may qualify as a *pretermitted heir*, a child born or discovered after the will was created and unintentionally left out. Oregon law does make exceptions in such cases."

Ryan absorbed that.

"So this doesn't automatically go to trial?"

"No. Probate disputes like this are typically handled by a judge, not a jury. Unless there's fraud, undue influence, or truly egregious behavior, most probate cases are bench trials, resolved in a courtroom, yes, but without the theatrics of a twelve-person jury." He paused.

"Frankly, contested estates are rare. Most wills go through without much fuss. But Caroline sees an opening, and she's exploiting it."

Ryan leaned forward. "What are we even fighting over? I haven't seen a dollar figure."

Mr. Graham opened a manila folder and tapped a few documents inside.

"Dalton left behind a sizable estate. A large property in Highland Park, high-end Dallas real estate. He was one of the top organ transplant surgeons in the country, a founding partner at the Dallas Surgical Group, and frequently gave keynote lectures and taught masterclasses across the country. His private jet wasn't just a toy; it was a business tool. The man built an empire of reputation and real estate."

He let that settle in before continuing.

"We don't have a hard number yet, but between investment accounts, medical practice equity, royalties from published research, the property, and his professional holdings, it's likely north of ten million dollars. And that doesn't include the life insurance."

Ryan blinked. "Ten million?"

"At least," Graham confirmed.

"And that's before taxes, fees, or any litigation carve-outs. He had reach, Ryan. Influence. And people like Caroline don't want to let go of a piece of that, even if they weren't central to his life."

Ryan exhaled slowly. "About the insurance policy…"

"Yes," Graham said, nodding. "I know. You mentioned it in your email. Two million. But the listed beneficiary was his late wife, and from what we've gathered so far, there was no contingent beneficiary named."

"So where does it go?"

"Without a valid beneficiary, it becomes payable to his estate, which makes it fair game for anyone involved in the probate process. Caroline will absolutely go after it. But that also strengthens your position as a presumptive heir."

"So this could get even messier."

Graham smiled grimly. "Welcome to probate."

Ryan rubbed his face. "We were just starting to connect. He wasn't just some stranger. He knew about me. Wanted me in his life."

"And that's the argument we build," Mr. Graham said, voice calm and sure. "Intent. That's everything. We'll document your internship at his clinic, your communications, and testimony from people like Sydney and Bill. If we can show he meant to include you, and simply didn't get the chance, it matters."

Ryan nodded. "I'll get you what I have."

"Good. Just remember, this isn't just about inheritance. It's about legacy. If Dalton's intent gets buried under paperwork and legal objections, it's his name that suffers, not just yours."

That afternoon, Ryan returned to the clinic, letting himself fall into the rhythm of patient visits. He needed normalcy. Arielle called between appointments, her voice light but pointed.

"So... how big is this estate supposed to be? I mean, that could really change things for you, especially if you're thinking about establishing roots in Shadow Bay."

Ryan hesitated. "They haven't put an exact number on it. But Mr. Graham thinks the estate's probably worth more than ten million. And that's without the insurance."

There was a pause. "Wow."

"It's complicated," Ryan added quickly. "Caroline's contesting it. And with the life insurance not updated, there's more on the line."

She exhaled on the other end of the line. "Are you still house hunting? Sydney's feels... awkward when I'm there. Especially with David always dropping in."

"I've got a couple of places to look at this week. Modest. I'm hoping for a yard."

"You still want a dog?"

"Always," he said, smiling despite himself. "I think I already have the name picked out."

That evening, the warmth of Sydney's log home offered an emotional reprieve. The scent of cinnamon rolls curled through the air, and Bill had stopped by too and was already settled in his favorite chair when Ryan walked in.

"Well?" Sydney asked, handing him a mug of hot cinnamon tea.

Ryan took the sofa.

"Graham thinks we have a solid shot. He believes I qualify as a *pretermitted heir*. And... the estate's larger than I imagined. Dalton had more going on than we realized. Property, medical holdings, research royalties. The house in Dallas alone could be worth several million."

Bill whistled. "That's a heavy stack of chips."

"And the insurance policy? Two million," Ryan added. "But his wife was still listed as the beneficiary."

Sydney's brow furrowed. "That makes things messy."

"It does," Ryan said. "If there's no alternate beneficiary, it becomes part of the estate, and that means more for Caroline to contest."

Bill leaned forward. "We'll help however we can, Ryan. But the more valuable the estate, the harder she'll fight."

Sydney reached for his hand. "Dalton meant to include you. We'll make sure that the truth is heard."

"Mom, I'll need you for your statements," Ryan said. "Especially since you knew Dalton before I did."

Sydney nodded. "Whatever it takes."

Ryan glanced toward the hallway. "Arielle wants me to move out soon. She's not comfortable here anymore."

Sydney offered a gentle smile. "I'll miss having you here. But she's right, you need your own space now."

"I want a yard," Ryan added. "And a dog."

Bill chuckled. "Smart man. A good dog won't ask for a cut of the estate."

The room warmed with a ripple of laughter, even as the weight of what lay ahead lingered just beyond the firelight.

Chapter 6 - State-of-the-Art

The clinic hummed with anticipation as construction on the new wing neared completion. Framed by vibrant evergreens and filled with streams of natural light, the expansion featured sleek, private suites, outfitted with cutting-edge technology tailored for neurology, hematology, diabetes management, arthritis treatment, and advanced memory care.

For Shadow Bay Medical Clinic, this marked the dawn of a bold new chapter, one that was ambitious, forward-thinking, and powered by AI innovation.

In the center of it all, David and Ryan moved between stations, tablets in hand, overseeing the rollout of *VitalMind*, the AI software David had designed. With each day, the system absorbed patient histories, lab trends, medication profiles, and physician notes. Dashboards sprang to life, visually mapping chronic conditions, projecting treatment efficacy, and flagging anomalies.

Ryan was fascinated by the power of the software. "This changes everything," he told David one afternoon.

"We're not just reacting anymore, we're predicting."

David nodded. "And learning from every patient encounter, whether it's ten years ago or ten minutes ago."

But as the old records were migrated into the new system, Sydney grew uneasy. Late one evening, she remained in her office, watching the lines of data populate *VitalMind's* backend. Her fingers hovered over the keyboard as her eyes narrowed on a flagged entry tied to John's chart, his last blood panel.

The markers looked familiar. Too familiar.

A shadow crossed her face as she leaned back in her chair. The AI was objective, indifferent, but relentless. It didn't forget the details. It didn't overlook any anomalies.

She closed the screen quickly as Ryan walked in with two mugs of tea. "You, okay?" he asked.

"Just tired," she said, forcing a small smile.

"This expansion is incredible. Overwhelming sometimes."

Ryan handed her the tea and sat across from her.

"You've built something important, Mom. People are going to come here from all over."

She nodded, but her eyes were distant.

The past had always lived quietly in the background. But now, it was waking up, digitized, sharpened, and increasingly unwilling to keep any past anomalies buried.

They shared a quiet laugh, the tension briefly easing as they prepared mentally for the challenges ahead.

As the conversation wound down, Ryan reached for his phone and glanced at the calendar. "Hey, are we still on for Taco Thursday this week?" he asked, flashing a hopeful grin.

Sydney smiled. "Of course. Unless you're too busy with your move?"

"Actually, that's part of why I asked," Ryan replied.

"I found a small place; clean, with a fenced yard. Just outside town, near the trailheads."

"That's great news, Ryan," Sydney said, her voice tinged with bittersweet pride.

"Yeah, I was wondering, would it be alright if I used the same cleaning lady you have?" he asked. "But there's a catch. I adopted a rescue, his name's Stix. He's about a year old, part husky, part lab. High energy, sweet-natured, but... a chewer."

Sydney grinned. "Sounds like you found yourself a sidekick."

"The neighbor kid is willing to check on him during the day, but with summer sports and all, there'll be days he can't. I'm trying to find someone who wouldn't mind helping with both cleaning and maybe just keeping an eye on Stix when I'm at the clinic or on call."

"We'll find someone," Sydney assured him. "Bring him by Thursday if you want. Just warn him about the furniture."

Ryan laughed. "Yeah, maybe I'll wait till he's out of his chewing phase."

Chapter 7 - Thirty Days

Bill had agreed to the terms with Valerie, one month. Thirty days to learn the vineyard, the margins, the risks, and Valerie.

Raincrest Cellars had charm, but charm didn't pay harvest loans or attract distributors. Bill wasn't here for sentiment. He was here to see if this was a business opportunity worth betting on.

Valerie handed him the keys to the east barn and a map of the blocks during their first morning debrief at sunrise.

"Don't worry about impressing me," she said, voice clipped from fatigue and hard work.

"Impress the vines. They're the ones that remember."

Bill liked that. She wasn't soft, not like she used to be when Mark ran the show and she stayed in the tasting room, smiling behind a wine-streaked counter. Mark was dead. Now Valerie ran every hose, every fermenter, and every crisis.

For two weeks straight, Bill worked alongside the hired hands, staking trellis posts, clearing underbrush, monitoring irrigation intervals, and checking Brix levels by mid-afternoon. Then, after dinner, he'd pull up a chair at Valerie's kitchen table with a glass of Pinot Gris and go over balance sheets, case sales, delivery invoices, and payrolls.

"This label's bleeding out cash," he muttered one evening, circling a margin in red.

"You've got good wine, but bad contracts. You're selling at bulk rates to restaurants that are barely moving volume."

Valerie crossed her arms. "Those buyers kept us afloat after Mark passed."

"I'm not judging the past," Bill said calmly.

"But if I'm going to be part of this, I need to know we can turn it around. And that I get a say in how."

She studied him, long and quietly. Then she nodded.

They met like that most nights, half business, half therapy. She confessed she hadn't opened the books fully to anyone since Mark died. Bill responded by pulling vineyard yield projections from old state ag reports and running them against their current output.

"You're getting seventy-five percent of what this land is capable of," he told her. "Even with good help."

That was when her expression changed. Wary. Hesitant.

"Cesar keeps the crews in line," she said, as if trying to convince herself. "They respect him."

"They fear him," Bill replied.

Valerie didn't argue.

It bothered Bill that nobody seemed to know who actually vetted the migrant workers. When he asked Valerie directly, she hesitated.

"That was always Mark's thing," she said, eyes falling to her coffee cup. "He had contacts. I trusted him to handle it."

Bill nodded, but he didn't like blind spots, especially not legal ones.

That weekend, under the pretense of needing fencing supplies, Bill took the long road through county backroads and stopped in at a modest brick building with an oxidized green sign that read: *Sheriff Howard Truman – Lane County.*

Sheriff Howard Truman had known Bill since their National Guard days. A man who aged into the uniform like it was a second skin, calm, dry-witted, and sharp enough to split hairs in a windstorm.

Sheriff Truman glanced up from the file he'd been pretending to read as Bill stepped into his office. The smirk forming on the sheriff's face was half amusement, half mischief.

"Well, if it isn't the talk of the town," Truman said, leaning back in his chair with a slow creak. "Word around the café is that you're making time with Valerie over at Raincrest. Some say it's the wine, some say it's the widow. What should I believe, Bill?"

Bill chuckled and shook his head.

"I'm not making time, Truman. I'm trying to make sense of her vineyard's books. She's got a decent operation, just not sure if it's salvageable or if Cesar's playing her sideways."

"Uh-huh," Truman drawled. "That's what every man says when he's about to go broke for a pretty woman with a business on the ropes."

He reached for his coffee, took a slow sip, then fixed Bill with a wry look.

"Let me give you some sheriff-approved wisdom, seeing as you're dancing close to the edge. Do you know the difference between complete and finished?"

Bill raised an eyebrow. "I'm listening."

Truman leaned in, lowering his voice like he was sharing a classified law enforcement secret.

"When you marry the right woman, you're complete. Marry the wrong woman, you're finished. But if you marry a woman who likes shopping... He paused, holding up a finger. "You're completely finished."

Bill burst out laughing. "Remind me not to take you shopping for rings."

"Just keep your wallet close and your heart closer," Truman said, then waved toward the chair across from his desk. "Now let's talk about those workers, legal status, paperwork, and what you might be walking into. So, you're giving up retirement and fishing duty now?" Truman said, pouring coffee from a chipped thermos into a styrofoam cup.

"Temporarily," Bill said, accepting the cup. "I'm helping Valerie Cavanaugh at Raincrest Cellars. I might be interested in a stake of the wine business."

Truman leaned back in his chair. "That vineyard needs more than help. It needs a priest."

Bill chuckled. "I'm trying to make sense of the crew. Most of 'em are good. But I need to know how to verify if they're here legally. Or if I'm stepping into a liability mess."

Truman's demeanor shifted, professional now. "You're asking good questions. To legally hire migrant or seasonal workers, you're supposed to go through the H-2A Program, a temporary agricultural visa. That means sponsorship paperwork, federal approval, and labor housing compliance. If they're local hires, you verify status with an I-9 form and either a permanent resident card, employment authorization, or a valid Social Security number."

"And what happens if none of that exists?"

"Then you've got a problem," Truman said. "First for employment violations, then for aiding and abetting if it's willful. ICE usually doesn't jump unless it's systemic, but if something violent or criminal comes up? You'll get the full spotlight."

Bill nodded. "Have you ever heard anything about Cesar or Luisa? "Quiet talk?"

Truman scratched his jaw. "Only that Cesar's name came up last year in an investigation involving another vineyard, Red Ridge Cellars.

Something about inventory theft and a crew dispute. No arrests. No proof."

Bill finished his coffee in silence, his jaw tight. "Howard," he said, standing up, "Off the record, if you found something like a tool possibly used in an assault, what would you do first?"

"Follow the blood," Truman said flatly. "Then decide whether you're dealing with an accident, negligence, or intent."

Bill thanked him and left.

By the third week, Bill started taking his own inventory. Fertilizer, sprays, and tools. It didn't always line up. Some invoices were inflated, especially from a regional supplier outside Eugene.

Luisa, always polite and prompt, provided digital copies on request. But they were too polished. Nothing scribbled. No driver initials. No drop-off times. Not even wine country ran that clean.

That afternoon, back in the tool shed while checking irrigation equipment, Bill found it. The pruning hook. Thick-handled, dull-edged, and caked with something dark, dry, and wrong.

He wrapped it carefully in a shop rag and later that night, using a syringe from his glove box first-aid kit, collected a dried sample. It went into a labeled vial, now tucked in the side pocket of his vest.

He'd take it to the medical clinic. Quietly, Ryan would know what to do.

He'd address it with Valerie when the time was right. He certainly wasn't going to mention the oleander clippings hidden in his shaving kit, either. That was a backup plan he'd brought with him, not as a solution, but a possibility. A dangerous one.

Some men packed just-in-case raincoats. Bill packed potential outcomes.

By week's end, the harvest sun had turned the skies over Raincrest Cellars the color of burnt honey. Valerie and Bill sat outside the main house, sipping a chilled glass of Chardonnay estate while looking out over Block 9.

"You've changed the tone around here," Valerie said. "There's order again. The books are better. The staff is...calmer."

Bill gave a slight nod. "But not Cesar."

"No," she said. Her voice lowered. "Not Cesar."

She swirled the wine in her glass but didn't drink it.

"I've never said this out loud," she continued. "Not even to the investigator when Mark died. But I've always had a gut feeling that Cesar had something to do with it."

Bill let the moment breathe. "Why didn't you press it?"

"No proof," she said, shaking her head. "And if I'd accused him, the crew would've walked. I couldn't lose them. I didn't know how to run the place on my own. Not back then."

"And now?"

"Now I don't care who walks away," she said softly. "If you've got something, if we can connect that tool to Mark's death, then I'll back whatever you decide to do."

"I've got the hook; I've got a blood sample from a pruning tool being tested."

Valerie's hand trembled slightly as she listened. "So, it wasn't just paranoia."

"No," he said. "It was instinct. You just didn't have anyone on your side."

She was silent for a long time. Then she looked at him, her voice low but steady.

"If the blood test comes back positive, what do we do?"

Bill didn't blink. "Then we move him out. Clean, quiet, and legal, if we can."

"And if we can't?"

Bill looked out at the vineyard, golden under twilight.

"Then we still move him out."

He didn't say anything more. He didn't have to.

Raincrest Cellars was still producing wine. But the real harvest was coming, *and it wouldn't be measured in cases or cash flow.*

Chapter 8 – Crushing Season

The vineyard was quieter than Bill expected for mid-harvest. A thick morning mist clung to the vines like a warning yet to be spoken. He zipped up his vest and stepped toward the barn, where Valerie was already loading the back of her pickup with crates for delivery. Her boots were caked in red soil, her eyes tired but alert.

"Start with Armando and Hector," she said, not looking up. "South slope. We're behind three days, and the buyers aren't going to wait."

Bill took the clipboard she handed him. "Still no update on the French oak shipment?"

Valerie exhaled through her nose. "Luisa says she's following up. But I don't trust the answers anymore."

Luisa, Cesar's wife, handled the front office, tastings, scheduled weddings, and harvest dinners, and even walked couples through barrel room vows and candlelit receptions. Her smile was always professional. Pleasant. But Bill had begun to wonder what lingered behind her eyes when no one was watching.

Cesar, meanwhile, spent his mornings in the fields and his afternoons near Valerie's shoulder, increasingly vocal about vineyard decisions. He wanted a partnership now, a stake in the operation. A future. But it wasn't offered, and Bill suspected he wasn't going to wait much longer for it.

Bill had hinted over the past weeks: the late shipments, the erratic finances, the unexplained gaps in payroll, the way Cesar had started whispering to the men in the bunkhouse at night. And Luisa? She always seemed to know what he would ask before he said it.

That night, over a bottle of estate Pinot, he brought it up.

"You think Luisa's too close to this?"

Valerie paused mid-pour. "What are you asking me?"

"She schedules every delivery, tracks every client, and walks the floor when you're gone. She knows the numbers. The accounts. Even the tank temperatures when they're adjusted after hours."

Valerie took a long drink. "And she's Cesar's wife. You think she'd sabotage me?"

"I think if something is happening under our noses, they'd be the two to manage it."

Valerie looked out the window, the vineyard barely visible beyond the porch light. "Considering what those two may be up to, how could Mark's passing possibly be an accident?"

"I think someone wanted you to believe it was an accident," Bill said softly.

At night, Bill slept in the bunkhouse near the workers. He kept to himself but listened. Some talked in hushed Spanish about past vineyards, others swapped rumors about ICE raids in southern counties. But one name kept coming up in tight tones: *Cesar.* Always with caution. Always with respect and fear.

Toward the end of the month, Bill walked into the shed again and noticed the pruning hook was not where he had left it.

That same day, Valerie handed him a glass of late-harvest Chardonnay during a slow hour in the tasting room. "Cesar said he wants to increase his hours. Claims he's owed more. He said he's keeping the crew from walking."

"Threat?" Bill asked.

"Warning," she replied.

Bill hesitated, thinking it best to keep the oleander option to himself.

Valerie stared at Bill.

"I haven't done anything," he said. "But I've thought about it."

Valerie looked perturbed. "Don't."

He nodded. "I won't. Not unless I have to."

The next evening, Bill spotted Luisa on the back patio after a client tasting. She was on the phone, pacing behind the barrel stacks, speaking in Spanish.

"...not yet. He suspects. We need to move fast."

She turned, startled when she saw Bill. Her face was perfectly pleasant again.

"Just confirming a caterer," she said in English, with a polished smile.

Bill returned the smile. "Hope it's not another one that cancels last-minute."

She didn't answer. Just walked away.

Raincrest Cellars was still turning grapes into wine, but beneath the tanks and behind the vines, something else was fermenting. Something dangerous.

Bill knew that the pruning hook had been used once.

He just didn't know who would be next.

Part III

Trials and Tribulations

Chapter 9 – Trial by Omission

The courthouse in Lane County was made of red brick and old ghosts. Sydney had passed it a hundred times but never stepped inside with her name on a docket. Now, her name was stamped in 12-point Times New Roman on a civil trial roster. *Binder v. Sydney Collins, A.P.R.N. & Shadow Bay Medical Clinic.* The clerk had already announced it twice that morning.

She sat stiffly at the defense table beside her assigned counsel, Victoria Stone from Harbor Point Indemnity's legal team — crisp, unshaken, and corporate to her marrow.

Victoria had read everything. She didn't blink when the plaintiff's attorney, Wesley Grant, walked in with a casual swagger and a six-figure suit, the kind of attorney who smelled like cologne, ambition, and daytime cable news.

Sydney's palms felt clammy despite the chill of the courtroom AC. She tried not to look toward Melanie Binder, seated just a few feet away, wrapped in a soft gray sweater and public sympathy. Her hands were folded tightly in her lap. No bandages. No visible scars. But her attorney had built a narrative that didn't require blood to show damage.

The jury was seated, six men, six women, all with the same unreadable expressions. Sydney tried to steady her breath as Victoria stood for the defense's opening statement.

"This case is not about a missed diagnosis," Victoria began, her voice even and unhurried.

"It's about refused care. It's about a patient who was given every reasonable opportunity to be evaluated for a rare genetic condition. And who declined."

She let the words settle. "Medical negligence is not a matter of hindsight or outcome. It is a matter of what was reasonable at the time. Ms. Collins documented her clinical judgment. Ms. Binder refused genetic testing. She declined multiple referrals. We have the notes. The signatures. The refusals."

Across the aisle, Grant scribbled with theatrical annoyance. Sydney couldn't tell if he was actually writing anything or just underlining adjectives in his own ego.

"And while the plaintiff may regret her decisions now," Victoria continued, "regret is not grounds for a civil penalty."

She sat down.

Wesley Grant rose slowly, one hand still resting on the edge of the table.

"Ladies and gentlemen of the jury," he said, his tone already low and intimate. "This is a story of assumptions. My client, a 33-year-old woman with a life ahead of her, trusted a medical provider to see beyond the obvious. To dig deeper. To protect her from the hidden risks in her very DNA."

He turned slightly toward Sydney. "But that didn't happen. And now Melanie lives with permanent cardiac damage. Because someone didn't push hard enough. Someone didn't insist. And that someone is seated here today."

Sydney didn't flinch. But something in her chest tightened. It wasn't guilt. It was fury. At how simple he made it sound. As if every patient came with perfect compliance and open doors.

That night, back in her clinic office, Sydney stared at her screen, long past visiting hours. The words *"Complaint for Medical Negligence"* were burned into her brain like acid on parchment.

She had spent twenty-two years building this clinic and its reputation, driving through storms to make house calls, staying late for working parents, combing through labs on weekends with a cup of cold coffee. Now, all of it was being reduced to bullet points on a legal exhibit.

The courtroom's buzz still echoed in her ears as she sat at her desk, shoes kicked off, trial binder laid out on her desk.

Her phone buzzed.

Ryan's text: **"Call me if you need to go over today's testimony."**

She didn't. Not yet. She already knew the defense would hinge on two things: the documented refusals and David's algorithmic breadcrumbs. They'd all gone over it twice before the trial even started.

David had met with her the past weekend, his brow furrowed behind his laptop, scanning every click, every access log Melanie had touched. He'd called it "predictive vindication," a way to map behavior against risk and intention.

"You didn't overlook her," he'd said. "She maneuvered around you."

While Ryan had been just as blunt. "This won't be about policy. It'll be about perception."

Now, after day one, the weight of it had settled, not as fear, but as clarity.

She would no longer defend her choices. She would explain them.

Let them ask.

She would answer.

All she had to do was outlast the next five days and face whatever came after.

Chapter 10 – The Weight of Judgment

The jury had been watching Sydney all morning. Some with folded arms, others scribbling notes, one older man nodding occasionally as if she'd already earned his trust. The court reporter clicked away rhythmically like a ticking explosive no one could disarm.

Victoria stood.

"Defense calls Sydney Collins, Advanced Practice Registered Nurse."

Sydney rose, smoothed her navy jacket, and took the stand. The microphone crackled as she settled in.

Victoria's tone was clinical, steady. "Ms. Collins, can you describe your first encounter with the plaintiff, Melanie Binder?"

"Yes," Sydney said.

"She came in for fatigue, bruising, and vague abdominal pain. Her bloodwork was unremarkable at first, but based on physical findings and vascular concerns, I raised the possibility of a connective tissue disorder. Specifically, Marfan or a vascular subtype of Ehlers-Danlos."

"And what did you do with that suspicion?"

"I recommended referral to neurology and cardiovascular genetics. Twice. Both were declined."

Victoria paced slightly. "Did the clinic have protocols in place for informed refusal?"

"We did. Still do. Melanie signed a declination form after each visit, and rescheduled twice after I flagged the risks in our EHR."

"Did you ever deny her care?"

"Never."

Victoria held up laminated copies of the signed declinations. "These were signed in front of you?"

"Yes."

"Did you pressure her? Intimidate her?"

"No," Sydney said, with steel beneath her voice. "I tried to inform her. She made her choices."

Victoria smiled faintly, then nodded toward the plaintiff's table. "No further questions."

Grant stood, slow and smooth, a courtroom cobra ready to strike.

"Nurse Collins," he said, his voice rich with manufactured concern.

"Are you a geneticist?"

"No."

"Do you hold a medical doctorate?"

"No."

"Then isn't it true you were operating outside your scope by even bringing up vascular Ehlers-Danlos?"

"No," Sydney said firmly. 'It is within my scope to raise differential diagnoses and refer out. Which I did."

Drexler narrowed his eyes. "But you didn't follow up after she declined. You let it go."

"I documented her decision, counseled her again at a follow-up, and documented that too."

"You knew she was at risk for arterial rupture."

"I knew there was a risk. I offered further care. She declined."

Grant stalked a few feet closer. "Isn't it true that you were overbooked that month? That the clinic had a staff shortage?"

Sydney's jaw tightened. "We were busy. But she received the standard of our care."

Grant paused, letting the tension hover. "And now... a young woman will live with a torn aorta and permanent vascular injury. But you're saying it's her fault."

"No," Sydney said softly. "I'm saying it wasn't mine."

Later that afternoon, Victoria stood again.

"Your Honor, the defense requests to recall the plaintiff for limited rebuttal questioning."

Grant objected. The judge overruled.

Melanie took the stand with the weary poise of someone rehearsed for sympathy.

Victoria approached.

"Ms. Binder, are you familiar with your patient portal on the Shadow Bay Clinic's Electronic Health Record System?"

"I am," Melanie said, guarded.

"Is it true that you accessed your visit notes from the prior year six times in the month before filing this suit?"

Melanie blinked. "I... I looked at them, yes."

"And is it true that you rescheduled your vascular referral appointments multiple times?"

"I had conflicts. Work. Travel."

"But you never kept one."

"No."

Victoria turned to the jury. "The defense introduces a behavioral pattern analysis from the clinic's AI-integrated EHR system, *VitalMind*, which flagged this patient as a *"risk minimizer."* The algorithm is designed to detect at-risk behavior, identifying Ms. Binder as likely to underreport symptoms and resist clinical escalation."

"Objection!" Grant barked. "Speculative! Unproven algorithm!"

"Overruled," the judge said. "Proceed, but keep it focused."

Victoria held up the printed metadata summary. "Ms. Binder, are you aware that this data indicates a behavioral pattern consistent with intentional avoidance of medical reality?"

Melanie's face flushed. "I didn't want it to be true..."

Victoria leaned in. "But when you realized it might be... you went looking for someone to blame."

Melanie's hands trembled. Her voice cracked. "I just didn't think it would get this bad."

Victoria's voice softened. "But that's not malpractice. That's fear. And fear doesn't make someone else negligent."

Silence. A long, heavy silence.

Closing Arguments

Grant painted a picture of a vulnerable woman misled by a system too busy to care.

"She came seeking answers," he said. "And was handed uncertainty. And when her body failed her, the clinic's protocols left her behind."

Then came Victoria's final strike.

"You have a decision to make," she told the jury.

"Not about sympathy, but about responsibility. Ms. Collins did what medicine demands: she informed, documented, and referred. She cannot be faulted because the patient chose not to listen. And you should not allow that fear to turn into a verdict that punishes the very people working tirelessly to care for this community."

Verdict

The jury deliberated for four hours. Long enough to feel dangerous.

Sydney sat next to Victoria, hands clasped, watching the door as if expecting ghosts to walk in.

At 5:11 p.m., the clerk stood.

"In the matter of Binder v. Collins and Shadow Bay Medical Clinic, we, the jury, find for the defendant on all counts. No damages awarded."

The courtroom held its breath for a beat.

Then Sydney closed her eyes, just once, and exhaled.

Wesley Grant slumped. Melanie stared straight ahead, blinking back something between confusion and grief.

Victoria squeezed Sydney's hand.

"You showed them," she whispered. "You didn't just defend your clinic. You defended what it means to care."

Chapter 11 – Back to Practice

The headline ran above the fold in the *Shadow Bay Ledger* the next morning:

"Local Clinic Cleared in Civil Suit: No Fault Found in Vascular Misdiagnosis Case"
By Mara Simons, Staff Reporter

Sydney didn't read the full article. She couldn't. She saw the photo, of her walking out of the courthouse beside Victoria, her chin lifted but her eyes tired, and pushed the paper aside as if it were something toxic.

The town would read it, of course. They'd talk. Some would see vindication. Others would see a near-miss. And a few, the ones who always grumbled about big-city medicine in small towns, wouldn't change their minds either way.

But the waiting room stayed full that day. And the day after. Patients still came.

Still trusted her.

That mattered.

Later that week, the clinic staff gathered in the upstairs breakroom, an unofficial debriefing fueled by store-bought pastries and tepid coffee.

"I was scared," confessed the receptionist, twisting her paper napkin. "I thought if they found you liable... I mean, would the clinic even survive something like that?"

Sydney gave a soft smile. "We all would've figured it out."

"But you didn't settle," said Maria, one of the Medical Assistants (MA). "That's what's so badass."

"I didn't settle," Sydney repeated, eyes on her coffee. "Because I knew I'd done everything I could. Not everything perfect. But everything right."

That night, she finally opened the drawer of her old secretary desk, the one with the secrets still hidden in its bottom compartment. She didn't touch the diary. Not yet. But the silence in her home felt different now.

Less threatening.

Ryan showed up unannounced three nights later, a six-pack in hand and his dog, Stix, at his heels.

"I've been too busy at work and with my new chewing addiction here. I haven't had much time to check and see how you are doing now that the lawsuit is in the books as a win," Ryan said, scratching the dog behind the ears.

"So... how are you actually?"

Sydney gave a dry chuckle. "Still upright. Still licensed."

Ryan smiled at Sydney. "You proved that empathy and evidence can co-exist. That we can fight to be right without forgetting to be human."

They sat on the back porch as the sun slid behind the trees. Stix chewed a tennis ball to death beside them.

Ryan finally broke the quiet. "You know... I've been thinking about Melanie."

Sydney turned.

"She wasn't malicious. She was scared. Her condition was real, even if the lawsuit shouldn't have been."

Sydney nodded slowly. "Fear makes people dangerous sometimes. Especially when they feel powerless."

Ryan looked at her. "We need to find a way to integrate *VitalMind* with more algorithms and build behavioral tracking into our triage workflows, and expand the toolbar menus. Not just for diagnosis, but for risk flags, and to reduce our human exposure to lawsuits. I'm getting efficient with VitalMind now that I've worked with David, picking his nerd brain. I think I can enhance the tool to better serve our medical procedures and reduce risk for not only us but the patients, too."

"I agree," Sydney said. "Let's enhance it. Quietly, without David. Test it first on internal cases."

Ryan smiled. "Taco Thursday next week? You owe Stix a plate."

Sydney smirked. "Only if he keeps his chewing to the plate."

Back at the clinic the next morning, Sydney stood in the new wing, the one they were still furnishing.

On the wall was a space marked for a framed quote she hadn't chosen yet.

She pulled out her phone, opened her notes app, and typed:

"Medicine isn't about being perfect. It's about being present, long enough, and hard enough, to matter when it counts."

She hit save.

Some battles weren't won in court.

They were won in the exam room where she chose to show up again.

Chapter 12 – Opening Arguments

The Lane County Courthouse didn't look like a battlefield, but Ryan Collins felt like he was walking into one. Room 3B had the sterile quiet of bureaucracy, but there was tension under the surface, an inheritance hanging in limbo, a name missing from a will, and a truth just out of reach.

Dr. Ryan Collins sat beside attorney William Graham, hands folded, heart thudding quietly under a tailored suit he wasn't used to wearing. Across the aisle sat Caroline Bade, dressed with the dignity of someone who'd practiced for this moment. Her attorney, Wendell Chase, shuffled his notes with an air of controlled disdain. The kind of man who sharpened technicalities into scalpels.

At 9:00 a.m. sharp, Judge Myra Thomas took the bench, lean, silver-haired, and sharp-eyed, with the poise of a woman who'd heard every kind of lie and still kept a half-open door for the truth.

"Call the matter," she said, her voice cutting cleanly through the air.

The bailiff stood. "In the matter of the Estate of Dr. Dalton Avery, Case No. 25-PR-1411, now before the Honorable Judge Myra Thomas."

"Proceed," she said.

Mr. Graham stood first, his voice calm, deliberate. "Your Honor, my client, Dr. Ryan Collins, is the biological son of the decedent, Dr. Dalton Avery. Though not named in the existing will, he qualifies under Oregon law as a *pretermitted heir*, a child unknown to the testator at the time the will was executed and not intentionally excluded."

He paused, letting the room settle.

"Dr. Avery's will, drafted nearly ten years ago, named only his wife, Abigail Avery, as the sole beneficiary. She predeceased him. With no codicil, no amendment, and no contingent beneficiary listed, the estate lacks a clearly directed succession. That leaves it open to lawful challenge."

Ryan's hands stayed still, but his jaw was tight.

Graham continued. "Dr. Avery was one of the nation's leading transplant surgeons, a founding partner in the Dallas Surgical Group, and a frequent speaker at national conferences. His estate includes a luxury residence in Highland Park, substantial medical equity, a private aircraft, investment accounts, and royalties from published clinical work. The total value is conservatively estimated at over ten million dollars."

He gave the briefest pause.

"And, newly discovered, there is a life insurance policy valued at two million dollars, which also lists Abigail as the beneficiary. As she is deceased, and no alternate was named, the policy is payable to the estate and thus falls under probate jurisdiction."

Judge Thomas made a note but said nothing.

"Finally," Graham said, his voice lowering, "we intend to show that Dr. Avery was flying to Oregon with his other son, Spencer, to visit Dr. Collins when the plane tragically went down. That trip, cut short by death, was meant to finalize what

Dr. Avery had already set in motion: a relationship with his son and, we believe, an amended legacy."

He returned to his seat with quiet gravity.

Wendell Chase rose next, his face impassive.

"Your Honor, while we do not dispute the unfortunate deaths involved, we caution the court against treating sentiment as a substitute for legal standing. Dr. Avery's will was clear. The sole beneficiary was Abigail Avery. With her gone, there is no expressed directive from the decedent to alter or redirect the estate."

He turned slightly, eyes glancing toward Ryan before returning to the bench.

"My client, Ms. Caroline Bade, is the decedent's niece and only surviving blood relation with a longstanding connection to the Avery family. She assisted Dr. Avery during his medical leave, maintained family trust accounts, and was an active part of his estate management discussions."

Ryan frowned. Discussions?

"We submit that Dr. Collin's claim, while biologically accurate, lacks the legal intent required for inheritance. No codicil. No posthumous letter. No confirmed declaration of support or recognition. This is not about blood; it is about paper. And the paper does not favor the petitioner."

Judge Thomas nodded once.

"Discovery motions?" she asked.

Graham stood. "We request all communications, emails, texts, estate memos, from the final eighteen months of Dr. Avery's life. Travel records. Clinic schedules. Internal notes from the Dallas Surgical Group. Financial summaries, insurance designations, and any correspondence between Dr. Avery and Ms. Bade regarding the estate or its structure."

Chase raised an eyebrow. "We object to that scope. Overbroad and invasive."

"Overruled," Judge Thomas said flatly.

"If the estate is in question, all relevant communications are discoverable. Produce the requested materials within ten business days."

Chase gave a stiff nod, lips pressed tight.

Judge Thomas removed her glasses and addressed the courtroom directly.

"This is a probate matter, not a popularity contest. The decedent is not here to speak, but the law provides ways to listen anyway. The petitioner claims intent through action. The respondent claims omission through silence. This court will weigh both."

She looked directly at Ryan. "Dr. Collins, you may not have had much time with your father. But this courtroom isn't interested in how long you knew him. It's interested in what he meant to do."

Then to both attorneys: "Preliminary evidentiary hearing is set for thirty days. Witness lists and motion schedules are due in two weeks. Dismissals will not be entertained before discovery is complete. Let's keep the motions sharp and the egos in check."

Her gavel struck once, firm and final.

"Adjourned."

Outside the Courthouse

Ryan stepped out into the chilled morning air, the clouds lower now, almost pressing against the city itself. He exhaled slowly.

Graham walked beside him in silence for a moment. "Chase is going to throw procedural sand in our gears. But that ruling? That was a good start."

"I keep thinking about what Dalton was going to say," Ryan murmured. "What he never got to."

Graham paused at the bottom step. "He tried. That plane trip was the loudest thing he ever said."

Ryan nodded, hands in his coat pockets, eyes on the horizon. "Then I'll be the echo."

Chapter 13 – Discovery

Three days after the initial hearing, William Graham received the first discovery package from Wendell Chase's office, four sealed boxes delivered by private courier, and a digital link to a secure server labeled *"Estate of Dr. Dalton Avery – Preliminary File Transfer."*

Dr. Ryan Collins stood in Graham's office overlooking downtown Shadow Bay, sipping lukewarm coffee while Graham's paralegal, Monica, clicked through the digital files.

"Most of this is boilerplate," Monica said, scrolling.

"Flight logs, financial account summaries, clinic meeting notes, the Dallas property records. And about a dozen PDFs of old correspondence from Dalton's medical lectures."

Ryan paced slowly behind her, glancing at Graham, who was on a speaker call with a title company trying to verify ownership of a second investment property.

Then Monica stopped.

"Wait, here we go."

She clicked open a two-page email thread dated six weeks before Dalton's death. The sender was *dalton.avery@dsghealth.org*, the official domain of the Dallas Surgical Group. The recipient? His estate planning attorney in Texas, a man named Braxton Mills.

Subject: "Urgent – Trust Formation for R.C."

Dalton Avery wrote: *Braxton, I've made a decision. I need to get something in place for Ryan Collins, the son I told you about. I'll be flying out to Oregon with Spencer in two weeks. I want to establish a trust for Ryan, medical education support, initial housing, and a stake in Sydney's Medical Clinic, if we can make that happen. Let's discuss structure and tax shelter options before I go. – D.A.*

Monica sat back. "This... isn't just casual correspondence."

Graham approached from behind, slowly removed his glasses. "No, it's not. It's intent. Pure and powerful."

Ryan leaned over her shoulder, reading it again. His throat tightened. "He was planning something permanent."

"Discovery gold," Graham muttered. "A trust, separate from the will, and right before the crash. Caroline's case hinges on the will being complete. This proves it wasn't."

Monica narrowed her eyes. "But here's the strange thing: there's no follow-up email. Dalton said he wanted to act before he flew out. That would've been two weeks. There should be something more."

Graham frowned. "Anything deleted?"

"Maybe," Monica said. "Hard to tell from the PDF copies they sent. But if this came from the original Outlook mailbox or server archive, there's usually a digital footprint. We'd need metadata to be sure."

She opened the file properties panel. "This was converted to PDF... two weeks ago. From Chase's firm."

Graham's voice darkened. "So, Chase had this. He knew."

Ryan turned to Graham. "You think he withheld something?"

"I think he cherry-picked. And if Dalton's attorney replied, and it's not in this production, we may have a bigger issue, discovery misconduct."

Graham picked up his phone and dialed.

Meanwhile – At Chase & Alder LLP, Portland

Wendell Chase closed his office door and tossed the remaining documents from the digital archive into the shredder tray. His associate, a younger attorney named Brett Combs, lingered near the doorway.

"You didn't include the Braxton response?" Brett asked cautiously.

Chase's jaw flexed. "No. That email speculated. The reply was ambiguous. We're not going to give Graham a fishing license."

"But,"

"It's not fraud," Chase snapped. "It's leverage. Let them dig. We'll stall. Let's keep the focus on the will. Abigail was the named beneficiary. No one else. That's the ground we fight on."

He glanced out the window toward the Willamette River. "But just in case, start backgrounding Ryan Collins again. Look for anything he wouldn't want aired in open court. Let's see how clean this new heir is."

Back in Shadow Bay – That Evening

The email had left Ryan rattled, but also strangely grounded. Dalton hadn't just thought of him. He had planned for him.

At Sydney's, the lights glowed softly from the kitchen as cinnamon tea steeped while Sydney read quietly in her chair.

Ryan stood in the living room, holding the printed email.

"He was trying," Ryan said quietly. "Right before they died. I wasn't just a surprise. I was... part of a plan."

Sydney stepped closer, reading the message over his shoulder. "He never got the chance to finish it. But that doesn't make it less real. What's Graham say?"

"We're filing a supplemental motion tomorrow. With this email, Chase must produce the rest, if there's more."

"And if there's not?" Sydney asked.

Ryan folded the printout slowly. "Then we subpoena Dalton's Texas attorney directly, and we ask why this wasn't in the original discovery."

Sydney nodded. "Such a mess for a legacy."

Ryan looked out toward the darkened backyard, already picturing the home he hadn't bought yet, the life Dalton had wanted for him, a life just out of reach, waiting for him to fight for it.

Chapter 14 - Motion to Compel

It was just past 8 a.m. when William Graham filed the Supplemental Motion to compel Full Discovery with the Lane County Probate Clerk. By noon, a hearing had been scheduled for the following morning, in chambers, at the request of Judge Myra Thomas.

The setting was intimate by courthouse standards. No audience gallery, no jury box. Just polished oak furniture, a white noise machine in the corner, and three people seated around a walnut conference table: Judge Thomas, William Graham, and Wendell Chase.

Dr. Ryan Collins sat silently against the back wall, permitted to observe but instructed not to speak unless addressed. He clasped the arms of the chair, watching his father's legacy get picked apart one phrase at a time.

Judge Thomas glanced over the printed email in front of her.

"You're certain this was not included in the original document production?" she asked.

Graham nodded. "Positive, Your Honor. This was buried in a larger batch of lecture files, without metadata, stripped to PDF. We only caught it through careful review. There's no email header, no reply thread, and no indication this came from a full server pull. We believe the defense selected what to turn over, while omitting potentially damaging material."

Chase adjusted his tie. "Respectfully, Your Honor, the email in question is speculative at best. It refers to an intention to consult. Not a signed trust. Not an actual legal document. And while it was inadvertently provided without additional context, there is no malicious intent here. We sent what we had."

"You sent what you chose to include," Graham said coolly.

"And you converted all emails to flat PDFs, eliminating timestamps, IP addresses, and delivery receipts. That's not good-faith compliance. That's redaction by formatting."

Judge Thomas raised her eyes. "Mr. Chase, you know better."

Chase didn't blink. "We acted within the scope of our interpretation of the discovery order."

"You acted within the scope of strategic ambiguity," Graham shot back. "There is almost certainly a response from Dalton's estate attorney, Braxton Mills. If Mr. Chase doesn't have it, he should say so under oath. If he does have it, then he has withheld a material piece of discovery."

Ryan could feel his pulse pounding.

Judge Thomas leaned forward, her hands folded. "Mr. Chase, do you have any correspondence from Braxton Mills or Dr. Avery that post-dates this email?"

Chase's eyes narrowed slightly. "We have no further documents we consider responsive."

"That wasn't my question," Judge Thomas replied, voice sharpened.

"Do you possess them?"

A long pause.

"We received additional emails in the archive, yes," Chase admitted. "But none that mention the petitioner directly."

Graham's eyes narrowed. "Then let's produce them, Your Honor. Let the court decide what's relevant. Not opposing counsel."

Judge Thomas nodded slowly. "So, ordered. Mr. Chase, you will deliver the complete and unedited email archive from Dr. Avery's email account, including all correspondence with Braxton Mills, within five business days. Format must include metadata, headers, and timestamps. No more PDFs. I want source files."

Chase looked like he'd swallowed a bitter pill but responded with a clipped, "Understood."

"Failure to comply," the judge added, "will result in sanctions, including the possibility of excluding your objection to Dr. Collins' standing outright. We're not going to play shell games in my courtroom."

With that, she stood, signaling the end of the conference. "This hearing is adjourned."

Hallway Outside the Judge's Chambers

Graham and Ryan walked in silence for several steps before Ryan spoke.

"She knew," he said, meaning Caroline. "She knew Dalton was planning something and still tried to erase me."

"She's not here to honor Dalton," Graham said. "She's here to claim what's left of him."

Ryan stopped at the window overlooking the courthouse lawn. "What happens now?"

"Now?" Graham said, slipping the court order into his briefcase. "We wait for Chase's next move. But I guarantee you, he won't go quietly."

Meanwhile, Caroline's Apartment in Dallas

"You're losing control of the narrative," Caroline Bade said into her cell phone, pacing the floor of her modern high-rise.

"That email should never have surfaced."

On the other end of the line, Wendell Chase swirled a glass of bourbon. "They caught it late. We didn't redact, just trimmed it."

"You need to do more than trim, Wendell. You need to bury him."

Chase exhaled. "Then we do it the old-fashioned way. We find a reason the court won't want him to inherit."

"And if there isn't one?"

Chase's voice lowered. "Then we make one."

Chapter 15 – Buried Truths & Manufactured Lies

Caroline Bade watched the raindrops race down her window in downtown Dallas, the skyline blurred behind the storm-glazed glass. Her phone lit up with a text:

"He's here."

She stepped away from the window and opened the door to a man in his late fifties. Lean, sharp eyes, black gloves, and a face that suggested he'd once had a badge, but left it under unpleasant circumstances.

Frank Merriman.

"Ms. Bade," he said, stepping inside without waiting for an invitation. "I reviewed the file. The kid's clean. No arrests, no rehab, no gambling, no lawsuits. Stanford grad. Hematology specialist. Cancer survivor, no less. Makes for a tough villain."

Caroline offered him a tight smile. "You didn't come here to admire him."

"No," Merriman agreed. "I came here to find pressure points. And with guys like this, you don't dig, you manufacture."

She handed him a flash drive. "Start with this: His Stanford thesis. There's a footnote discrepancy on page 47, an uncited reference to a Canadian study. Minor, but enough to file an academic inquiry. I want it flagged with Stanford's ethics board."

Merriman raised an eyebrow. "That'll take weeks."

"Good," Caroline said.

"Because in the meantime, Chase's legal team will subpoena Stanford for his academic records. If there's even a whisper of impropriety, we can argue credibility issues in court. Judges don't like uncertainty."

Merriman pocketed the drive. "And if the inquiry clears him?"

Caroline's smile didn't reach her eyes. "Then we've still forced him to defend his past instead of focusing on the case. Distraction is leverage."

Two Days Later – Shadow Bay Medical Clinic

Dr. Ryan Collins sat across from Graham in the attorney's office, gripping a freshly served subpoena.

"Stanford?" Ryan frowned.

"Why would Chase's team care about my grad school records?"

Graham exhaled sharply. "Because they're looking for anything to muddy your reputation. If they can suggest you've misrepresented yourself, even academically, they can plant doubt in the judge's mind."

Ryan leaned forward. "There's nothing to find."

"Doesn't matter. The threat of something is enough to stall proceedings. And if they delay long enough, Caroline could push for interim control of the estate."

Ryan's jaw tightened. "Good God, what do we do?"

Graham slid a folder across the desk. "We counterattack. Braxton Mills's deposition is in two days. If he confirms Dalton was serious about the trust, and that Chase knew, then Caroline's entire claim unravels."

Dallas, Texas – Elsewhere

Frank Merriman sat in a back booth of a dimly lit diner, flipping through Ryan's academic file. His burner phone buzzed.

Unknown number:
"Ethics inquiry filed. Stanford will notify him within 48 hours."

Merriman smirked and sipped his coffee.

Let the kid sweat.

Chapter 16 – The Deposition

The law offices of Mills, Callahan & Moore sat high above downtown Dallas in a tower of reflective glass. Dr. Ryan Collins sat quietly in the conference room, flanked by William Graham and his paralegal Monica, who was already setting up her laptop and small digital recorder.

Across the long mahogany table sat Braxton Mills, Dalton Avery's longtime estate attorney, tall, salt-haired, and dressed like he'd just walked out of a blue-chip investment meeting. His expression was neutral, but his eyes flickered to the folder in front of him more than once.

The deposition was given under oath, recorded on video, and transcribed.

The court reporter adjusted her mic. "This is the deposition of Braxton Mills in the matter of the Estate of Dr. Dalton Avery. Counsel, please proceed."

William Graham leaned in, voice steady. "Mr. Mills, how long did you serve as Dr. Avery's attorney?"

"Roughly fifteen years," Mills replied.

"I handled his estate planning, tax structuring, partnership contracts, and several property acquisitions."

"Did you revise his will during that time?"

"Twice. Most recently in 2015. That version named his wife, Abigail Avery, as sole beneficiary."

"And after Abbey's death?"

Mills's jaw tensed. "We discussed making changes. But nothing was executed."

Graham lifted a page. "Your Honor, I'd like to enter Exhibit 12, an email from Dr. Avery to Mr. Mills, dated six weeks prior to his death. The subject line reads, *'Urgent – Trust Formation for R.C.'*"

He passed a copy across the table. "Mr. Mills, do you recall receiving this?"

"I do."

"In that email, Dr. Avery asks you to begin the process of forming a trust for his son, Ryan

Collins, my client, prior to flying to Oregon to visit him. Did you reply?"

Mills hesitated, then nodded. "Yes. I did."

Graham tapped his pen. "Please describe the contents of that reply."

"I confirmed receipt and advised him that we could begin the structure immediately if he provided the details I requested: trustee preferences, asset contributions, intended duration, and any stipulations. I also offered to schedule a call."

"Did that call take place?"

"No. His assistant emailed me two days later, canceling the call due to travel prep. We never spoke again."

Graham paused. "To your knowledge, did Dr. Avery ever revoke his intent to establish the trust?"

"No. He seemed eager. It was a priority."

"And yet," Graham said slowly, "that reply, your email, was not included in the discovery materials submitted by counsel for Caroline Bade. Can you explain that?"

Mills looked slightly uncomfortable. "No, I can't. I submitted my full archive when requested."

Monica looked up from her screen. "Metadata from your email server shows your response was sent within twenty-four minutes of Dr. Avery's original email. Which raises the question, why was it missing from the defense's production?"

Across the table, Wendell Chase cleared his throat. "Objection. This line of questioning suggests misconduct without evidence."

Graham didn't flinch. "Just asking why the most critical email in establishing intent was omitted."

Judge Thomas wasn't present, but the court reporter paused, sensing the weight in the room.

Graham returned to Mills. "Did Dalton Avery ever mention Caroline Bade as an intended beneficiary after Abbey's death?"

Mills shook his head. "Not once. He considered her distant family. Respectable, but not part of his estate plan."

"So, in your professional opinion, was Dr. Avery's intent to bring Ryan Collins into his estate legitimate and actionable?"

Mills looked across the table directly at Ryan for the first time.

"Yes. It was real. He told me, *'He's my son, and I want to give him a future.'* I believed him. And if that plane hadn't gone down, we wouldn't be sitting here today."

Silence settled over the table.

Graham nodded. "No further questions at this time."

Outside the Law Offices – Parking Garage

Ryan leaned against the cold cement wall, the air heavy with diesel and distant city noise.

Graham joined him. "We've got intent. From the only man who knew for sure."

Ryan exhaled. "So, we win?"

"Not yet," Graham said.

"But today, we just kicked Caroline out of the driver's seat."

He looked back toward the elevators. "Now we see how she handles losing control."

Chapter 17 – The Unraveling

The phone call came just after midnight.

Caroline Bade sat alone in her Dallas condo, the glow of her TV flickering across untouched wine and an open laptop. She didn't bother turning down the volume as Wendell Chase's voice crackled through her speaker.

"It's done," he said.

"Mills's deposition confirms everything. Dalton was setting up a trust. His intent was clear. And Judge Thomas isn't going to need a trial to see it."

Caroline didn't respond at first. Her fingernail scratched nervously along the stem of her glass.

"She'll issue a bench ruling," Chase continued.

"Probably within a week. We're out of options, Caroline."

Her voice was ice. "No, we are not. I want you to contest Mills's credibility."

Chase sighed. "He's a thirty-year estate attorney with impeccable standing. And his metadata files matched the server timestamps. If I challenge him now, I risk sanctions or worse."

"You don't walk away," she snapped.

"I don't, but I know when to stop swinging. The will named Abbey. She's dead. There's no codicil. No alternate beneficiary, and now you've got the son Dalton flew across the country to see, backed by an email and a deposition. The law is against us."

"So... what now?" she said, quietly furious.

Chase paused. "Now, we mitigate."

Portland – Offices of Chase & Alder LLP

Chase poured himself a drink and stared out at the Willamette River. His junior associate, Brett, lingered in the doorway.

"She's threatening to go public," Brett said.

"Media interviews, personal memoir, and claims of being erased by the Avery estate."

"She'll only humiliate herself," Chase said. "But let her vent. If it makes her feel powerful, fine."

"Should we prepare for post-ruling negotiations?"

Chase turned. "No, there won't be any. Once Judge Thomas rules, the Avery estate is Dr. Ryan Collins' legacy. All that's left for Caroline is a polite way to step aside."

Lane County Probate Court – One Week Later

The filing arrived on a gray Friday morning in Graham's inbox. It was short. Decisive. Issued under seal for now.

ORDER OF FINAL DISTRIBUTION – IN RE: ESTATE OF DR. DALTON AVERY

The court, having reviewed all submitted materials, depositions, and sworn testimony, finds that the decedent, Dr. Dalton Avery, demonstrated clear and convincing intent to provide for his biological son, Dr. Ryan Collins, as a legal heir to his estate.

As the sole remaining legal descendant, and in light of the will's original beneficiary (Abigail Avery) being deceased, the court hereby recognizes Dr. Ryan Collins as the rightful successor to the entirety of the estate, inclusive of all assets, holdings, and insurance policies defaulted to probate.

No further hearings will be scheduled.

– Hon. Myra Thomas, Presiding Judge

Later That Night – Sydney's House

The fire crackled quietly in the hearth as Bill poured two glasses of whiskey. Ryan sat with the envelope in his lap, unopened for the third time.

"You going to read it or just admire the seal?" Bill asked.

Ryan peeled it open, scanned the page again, then exhaled hard. "It's over."

You sure?" Bill asked.

"No," Ryan said honestly. "But it feels like he's finally heard."

Sydney walked in with a plate of peeled shrimp and cocktail sauce, her smile soft but full.

"You earned that ruling," she said.

"With dignity, not drama."

Ryan nodded. "Dalton didn't get to change his will. But he changed his course. And that... was enough."

They clinked glasses quietly.

Outside, the Oregon rain tapped softly at the windows, but inside, legacy finally found its rightful heir.

Chapter 18 – A New Wing, A New Name

The last box had been unpacked, and Ryan Collins stood barefoot in his new living room, finally still. The house was just outside Shadow Bay, two bedrooms, a fenced yard, and quiet evenings broken only by the occasional bark of his half-husky rescue, Stix.

From the hallway came a sudden thud.

"Stix?" Ryan called out.

The dog danced in with a guilty look and the corner of a bath towel trailing from his mouth.

Ryan chuckled and took it from him gently. "We'll get you trained before you destroy my decor."

He looked around, paint fresh, furniture minimal, and sunlight pouring in through west-facing windows. For the first time in months, maybe years, life felt like it was moving forward.

Later That Week – Shadow Bay Medical Clinic

The clinic's newest expansion, a state-of-the-art wing for diagnostic services and chronic care, was up and running. Eight fully equipped patient suites, advanced hematology and neurology diagnostics, and upgraded treatment rooms for diabetes, arthritis, and memory disorders had transformed Shadow Bay's small-town clinic into a regional medical anchor.

It had all come together on schedule: the walls painted, the equipment calibrated, the staff in place. But one thing was still missing.

"It needs a name," Sydney said during their weekly partner meeting, held in the glass-walled conference room that overlooked the new wing.

"A space this important deserves more than a room number and a floor plan."

Ryan glanced up from his notepad. "I was hoping you'd consider naming it after my father."

Sydney tilted her head slightly, already expecting the request.

"He was preparing to become part of this place," Ryan continued.

"Even if he didn't make it, this clinic was something he believed in, because I was part of it. Naming the wing after him feels... right. Not for me, but for the legacy he never got to finish."

Bill gave a slow, approving nod. "I second that."

Dr. Bell leaned back in her chair. "I think we all do."

Sydney looked around the table. No objections. Just quiet assent.

"Then it's settled," she said.

"We'll have the plaque ordered and the naming filed with the state health registry."

Later That Day – Financial Office

Bill met privately with Ryan after the meeting. He placed a slim folder on the desk between them.

"My vineyard days are pulling more of my attention, and Valerie could use the help. I'd like to offer you the chance to buy a portion of my silent partnership shares. It's time you had more say around here."

Ryan opened the folder. "Seriously?"

Bill smiled. "You're not the new guy anymore. You're the next generation."

The offer was generous, reasonable, and symbolic.

"I'll take it," Ryan said. "And I'll make sure this place grows the right way."

One Week Later – Dedication Ceremony

A modest crowd gathered beneath the spring sun. A short stage stood at the clinic's main entrance, flanked by two simple planters. Sydney stepped to the microphone first, thanking the partners, the staff, and the community.

Then Ryan took the stage.

"I never had the opportunity to work as a doctor side by side with my father. But I know what he valued: commitment, medicine, and building something that outlives you. This wing does that. For him, for all of us."

The canvas covering the new signage was pulled away to reveal the engraved steel:

The Dr. Dalton Avery Center for Precision Medicine - *In honor of a legacy unfinished but never forgotten.*

Ryan looked out over the crowd: colleagues, patients, and friends. This wasn't about inheritance anymore. It was about what you do with what you're given, and who you choose to become because of it.

Part IV

Quiet Roots, Deeper Soil

Chapter 19 – Beneath the Vines

Ryan's text came in just after dawn: "A+ human blood. No way to confirm identity without a tissue match. Careful with this."

Bill read it twice, then locked his phone and slid it into his jacket pocket. He stood at the edge of the vineyard, boots sunk into damp loam, watching steam rise off the irrigation channel as if the earth were exhaling secrets.

It wasn't enough to convict. Not by a long shot. But it was enough to convict *him*, in his gut.

Mark's death had never sat right. Now it had a direction. A blade, a blood type, and Bill, for better or worse, had a plan.

He returned to the house midmorning to find Valerie slumped over the kitchen counter, a damp towel pressed to her forehead and a bottle of ibuprofen beside her.

"Migraine?" he asked gently.

"Three days running," she murmured. "Luisa called in sick today. Cesar's nowhere to be found. Two suppliers are holding shipments because their payments bounced. I checked the books. They've been bleeding me, and I didn't see it."

Bill poured her some cold water and set it in front of her.

"You didn't want to see it," he said. "But that ends now."

She looked up at him, pale but fierce. "If you're thinking about going to the sheriff, don't. That blood test won't hold up. Not in court."

"I know," Bill replied, his voice calm. "But court's not the only place justice is served."

She held his gaze for a long time, then turned away. She didn't ask what he meant. She didn't need an answer.

Cesar had been avoiding him. That was fine. Bill used the time to plant the story, subtle and quiet.

At lunch with a few of the pickers, he dropped a comment about ICE raids at Red Ridge and Fox Hollow. That the sheriff was asked to pull employment files for vineyards with questionable hiring records. That Raincrest might be next.

By the next morning, Cesar was gone.

His truck disappeared. His tools were left behind. Luisa looked stunned. She made a few calls. Left a voicemail or two, then announced to Valerie and Bill that he'd fled because of ICE.

"Probably heading back to Mexico," she said, almost proudly. "Didn't even say goodbye."

Bill just nodded.

Luisa didn't ask any questions. Probably because she already knew too many.

The night Cesar "disappeared," Bill had waited for hours until the property was perfectly still. He knew Cesar had no papers—an undocumented presence invisible to official records, leaving no breadcrumbs to follow. Without a birth certificate, driver's license, or tax record, Cesar's sudden absence would hardly register beyond local gossip. It was precisely this invisibility that Bill had counted on.

When the last light faded from the farmhouse windows, Bill backed the skid steer quietly into the lower fields, guiding it to the secluded spot where a secondary irrigation trench had been dug the previous spring but never connected. Deep and remote, hidden in shadows and already partially filled with silt, it was an ideal grave, a place that would keep its secret.

The wine was a carefully selected blend, a Raincrest reserve no longer available for sale. Crushed oleander leaf and bark had been methodically infused into the bottle. It was potent enough to mimic a violent stomach flu at first, subtle enough to conceal its lethal intention, yet powerful enough to stop Cesar's heart by morning.

Earlier that day, after a tense exchange, Bill had offered Cesar the tainted bottle as a gesture of reconciliation. Cesar, unaware and grateful for the supposed truce, had accepted. Later, Bill watched quietly from a distance under the floodlights as Cesar drank deeply. Then, patiently, Bill waited.

Three hours later, it was done.

The trench accepted the body silently and without resistance. Bill methodically smoothed and leveled the earth with the skid steer bucket, tamped the disturbed soil carefully, and then planted dormant grape starts atop the fresh grave.

By sunrise, only earth, vines, and silence remained.

The chaos that followed was manageable. In Luisa's version of events, Cesar fled to avoid arrest. She cried a little. Not too much. She seemed more concerned about how to cover the weekend wedding tastings without him helping with the kids.

What she didn't expect was Bill going through the books, line by line.

Invoices for double shipments. Phantom service calls. Markups on fertilizer that never arrived. And every one of them signed off by Luisa.

Valerie was too sick to catch it right away. She was pale, groggy, and distracted. She blamed stress. Bill blamed betrayal.

By week's end, Bill confronted Luisa in the cellar office.

"You and Cesar skimmed from every angle," he said flatly.

"And if I run this audit through an audit accountant, your name's on every dotted line."

Luisa turned pale. "You don't understand, he made me. He said Mark owed him."

"Mark's dead," Bill cut in.

"And you're about one lie away from losing everything."

She slumped into the desk chair. "What do you want?"

"I want you gone. Quietly, no fuss. You leave this place and don't come back."

"You'll never prove any of it."

"I don't have to," he said. "But I'll make sure every vendor in the valley knows your name, and I'll mention the IRS. Trust me, they care a lot more about receipts than I do."

Luisa left before dawn two days later. No notice. No forwarding address.

Bill watched her car kick up dust as it vanished down the gravel road. Then he turned back toward the house, where Valerie lay curled on the couch, a cold compress over her eyes and unopened mail piling at her feet.

He picked up the mail, tossed the junk, and placed the rest on the coffee table.

"Rest," he said.

"I've got the vineyard."

She murmured something, but Bill was already gone, headed for the crush pad, where the grape processing begins, with clipboard in hand.

Raincrest Cellars wasn't whole yet, but it was finally under control.

Chapter 20 – Too Many Questions?

The call came just after eight.

"Bill," Ryan said. "You got a minute?"

Bill was already in the field by then, clipboard in hand, scribbling down estimates for next season's trellis repairs.

"Always," he replied. "What's going on?"

"The blood sample was human, same type as Mark's. No animal contamination. But... there's no way to prove conclusively it's his. Legally, it's not enough.

Bill already knew that from Ryan's earlier text. Still, hearing it out loud closed a door. And opened another.

"You said you got it off a tool?"

"Yeah," Bill said. "Found it in the shed. Covered. Hidden."

There was a pause. Then Ryan's voice dropped half a tone.

"You still want me to destroy the sample and scrub the report?"

"I didn't say that," Bill replied. "Just... keep it between us."

Another pause.

"Okay," Ryan said. But his tone wasn't in agreement. It was a note of something else, unease. Maybe mistrust.

Bill hung up and stared out over the east blocks. The soil looked calm. Innocent. But that was the thing about dirt, it covered everything.

Sheriff Truman's truck kicked up dust as it rolled into the gravel drive just after lunch. Bill saw it from the crush pad and met him halfway, wiping his hands on a rag that still smelled faintly of ferment.

"Didn't know I was expecting company," Bill said.

"Wasn't planning on making house calls," Truman replied, stepping down.

"But heard something this morning at the café."

Bill raised an eyebrow. "You're going to have to narrow that down. Those ladies love a story."

Truman grinned. "Something about Cesar and Luisa. Disappearing. One gone in the night, the other gone without warning."

"Cesar left the crew," Bill said casually.

"Didn't give notice. Luisa got caught cooking the books. Valerie let her go. Pretty straightforward."

"Maybe," Truman said, brushing dust from his vest. "But I remember when straightforward meant boring. This one doesn't feel boring."

Bill motioned him toward the shade of the press deck. "You here in an official capacity?"

"Not yet," Truman said. "Just coffee, donuts, and old instincts."

They stood in silence for a moment, watching a tractor roll by in the distance.

"You seen Cesar?" Truman asked.

"Not since the day before he left."

"And you didn't find it strange he bailed right after the ICE buzz started flying?"

Bill shrugged. "Sometimes the truth motivates people more than a threat. He wasn't legal, was he?"

Truman's silence confirmed enough.

"He was also smart," Truman said. "Didn't leave a trail. No word. No forwarding contact. No personal effects from the bunkhouse."

"He traveled light," Bill said.

Truman studied him. "You ever hear of a man leaving behind his boots?"

Bill didn't answer.

The silence stretched. Then Truman sighed and shifted his footing.

"You've always been a man of action, Bill. Don't let that get confused with being above the law."

"I know where the line is," Bill replied.

"Good," Truman said. "Because I got two different stories from two different people about what happened out here. Valerie's holding it together with aspirin and bravado. You're managing the books and the crews. And somehow, everything just got easier after Cesar left."

Bill didn't blink. "Sometimes subtraction's the solution."

Truman nodded slowly. "If Cesar shows up dead, I'm coming back with more than donuts."

"I'd expect nothing less."

They stood there for another breath, and then Truman turned to leave.

"Oh," he added, halfway to the truck, "Ryan's a good kid, bright. Doesn't miss much. You might want to keep him in the loop before he starts putting pieces together on his own."

Then he was gone.

That night, Bill sat alone at the edge of the vineyard with a glass of wine and the kind of silence that didn't comfort.

Ryan hadn't said it, but the tone in his voice that morning had shifted. He was suspicious. Not yet certain. But moving toward it.

And Truman? He hadn't come to chat. He'd come to warn.

The problem wasn't what Bill had done.

It was how many people might start with more questions than answers.

Chapter 21 - One Last Pour

The smell of the evergreens and the faint whiff of Lemon Pledge from Sydney's secretary desk filled the living room as rain tapped softly against the custom log home's oversized windows. David sat across from Sydney on the leather sofa, a tumbler of Raincrest Cellars' Pinot Noir in hand, swirling it more than sipping. His usual certainty had given way to something quieter, more restrained.

"I got the call this morning," he said, not meeting her eyes.

Sydney looked up from her clinic notes. "From whom?"

"Zurich. It's a private medical consortium. They're funding a project on AI-driven diagnostics for rare diseases. Real-time genome analysis, patient-side integration. Everything I've dreamed about, except they actually have the budget to make it happen."

She set her pen down. "Switzerland."

David finally met her gaze. "Six months minimum. It could be two years. They want me to lead it."

The room fell silent except for the ticking of the grandfather clock, which Bill had insisted gave the place character. Sydney tried to smile, but her chest felt heavy. "I'm proud of you. I really am."

"I'd ask you to come, Syd, but I already know the answer." He gave a short laugh, more sad than amused.

"You've got the clinic, the town, Ryan, and Bill. Your roots are here."

"And your branches were always meant to reach further," she said softly.

They sat in the quiet, sipping wine that suddenly tasted bittersweet. David leaned forward, elbows on his knees. "Part of me wants to say no to all of it. But... this is the kind of work I've waited my whole career to do."

"You don't have to explain," she said, touching his hand. "You never did."

He lingered for another hour, helping her box up old files and transfer clinic notes into the *VitalMind* dashboard, a symbolic farewell chore. When he finally stood to leave, he paused at the door.

"If you ever do decide you want out of Shadow Bay for a while," he said. "There's a place for you in Zurich, and in my life."

She nodded, her eyes dry but burning. "Safe travels, David."

As the door clicked shut, Sydney turned toward the darkening vineyard hills, the reflection of her face faint in the window glass. She whispered, "Goodbye," to a man who had offered everything she couldn't take and taken nothing she wasn't willing to give.

- Loose Ends -

It was Saturday, and the coffee pot hissed with a rich dark roast, resulting in a bold, rich flavor with notes of chocolate, caramel, and nuts. Sydney stood barefoot near the sink, cradling her favorite oversized mug. Ryan, popped in fresh off an early morning run with Stix and still damp from a quick shower, pulled up a stool at the kitchen island.

"Smells like you're brewing peace treaties again," he said, nodding at the coffee.

"Something like that," Sydney murmured. "David left this morning."

Ryan raised a brow. "What? That fast?"

"Zurich. AI fellowship. Leading a multi-national team. It's the kind of thing he's always wanted." She paused, looking down into her cup. "It just came on so... clean. No discussion, no offer to pivot remotely, nothing. Like he'd already decided."

Ryan leaned in slightly, his easy smile fading. "That doesn't really sound like him."

"I thought so too." She exhaled, setting her cup down.

"He said he got the call yesterday morning, but I saw his passport on the entry table two days ago. He'd already renewed it."

Ryan frowned, connecting a few dots. "So he didn't just get the call, he was expecting it."

"Or orchestrating it," she added, then shook her head.

"No. That's unfair."

Stix let out a soft whine and nuzzled Ryan's leg, sensing the tension. Sydney looked out the window where the dog had left muddy paw prints on her new patio stones. She didn't even care.

"Maybe I'm just tired," she said. "Too many moving parts lately. The clinic. The malpractice suit. The wing expansion."

Ryan sipped slowly, watching her. "Or maybe your gut's talking again. It's not wrong very often."

"I don't know what I'm accusing him of, Ryan. He just... left. But part of me thinks that project in Switzerland, well-funded, high-profile, was waiting for the right reason to become urgent."

Ryan tilted his head. "And maybe you, or the clinic, were part of the package deal that made his résumé shine a little brighter."

Sydney didn't respond. She didn't need to. The silence between them was answer enough.

He stood and kissed the top of her head gently. "If there's more to it, it'll surface. They always do. For now, I think you're better off not dragging uncertainty into your next chapter."

She nodded slowly, her eyes locked on the morning fog rolling down the hillside like a curtain between her and something she hadn't yet seen clearly.

Chapter 22 – Fault Lines

Arielle stood on the back deck of Ryan's A-Frame home, the early autumn sun catching flecks of gold in her hair as she scrolled through emails. Below, Stix bounded across the yard in wild loops of joy, dragging a deflated soccer ball like it was treasure.

She sipped from her coffee and sighed.

Ryan stepped out with two mugs and offered her a refill. "He's obsessed with that thing."

"I can tell," she said, deadpan. "I've been watching him chew it for the last thirty minutes."

Ryan grinned. "Come on, admit it, he's growing on you."

"He's growing on my shoes."

Stix barreled toward the deck steps and flopped with a thud, panting and proud.

Arielle raised an eyebrow. "How long before he realizes Palo Alto doesn't have yards like this?"

Ryan didn't answer right away. She knew why.

That afternoon, they drove into town for lunch at the Shadow Bay Market Café. It was quaint, with chalkboard menus and mismatched chairs, and two elderly women exchanging gardening tips by the window. Arielle looked politely amused but wildly out of place.

She had her laptop out before dessert, skimming through reports from her biotech firm. She'd been working on a patent-supporting antibody development project, a big one, potentially IPO-bound. Ryan respected her drive. He always had.

But over lunch, the differences surfaced again.

"I got a call from the clinic board," Ryan said. "They're backing my proposal to expand the hematology program. I'm buying out a bigger share from Bill. The new wing's already named after Dalton."

"That's great," she said. Her voice didn't match her words.

"You don't sound thrilled."

"I am. It's just... permanent. Like this place is swallowing you up."

Ryan tilted his head. "You knew I planned to stay here after graduation."

"You were going to weigh your options. You didn't mention becoming a major partner or planting your roots in the middle of nowhere with a dog and a file cabinet full of town secrets."

He leaned back in his chair. "You think I should've moved back to Palo Alto."

"I think you've forgotten how ambitious you used to be."

Ryan didn't respond.

They sat in silence as Stix, tied to a post outside, barked happily at a leaf blowing in the wind.

That night, after a long walk near the lake, Ryan stoked a fire and poured two glasses of Pinot Noir.

Arielle was seated on the floor, legs crossed, reading something on her phone.

"Investor updates?" he asked.

"Sort of."

He waited.

Finally, she said, "There's a lot of chatter about my company acquiring a smaller diagnostics lab, Hemovein. They do some bloodwork analytics, AI-based flags for abnormalities. It's pre-IPO, very hush."

Ryan's ears perked. "You're working with them?"

"I know the founder," she said, carefully. "From grad school."

Ryan took a slow sip of wine. "Is this the same company that pitched their software to Stanford last year?"

She nodded. "They had a few red flags then, but they've cleaned most aspects up."

"Ryan, if you're thinking what I think you are, don't. They're not the kind of people you want to compete against. And *VitalMind*, David's software? They've probably already studied it. Quietly."

Ryan set his glass down. "That's not what you said six months ago."

"That was six months ago," she said.

"Before you had your own clinic. Before you had something to lose."

He looked at her, his eyes narrowing slightly.

"What's really going on, Arielle?"

She hesitated, then replied. "Nothing. Just...don't be naive. Shadow Bay may be quiet, but biotech isn't."

Later, when Ryan stepped into the kitchen to clean up, Stix nosed a tote bag Arielle had left by the door. Something fell out, a slim, hardbound notebook. Not her journal. Not a lab notebook. Something else.

He picked it up and saw the label: "Interview Notes – Spechaven Diagnostics Proposal – CONFIDENTIAL"

Ryan's brow furrowed. Spechaven Diagnostics was a shell company; one he remembered hearing about during the AI trials that David had once flagged as *corporate camouflage for competitor intel gathering.*

He put the notebook back where he found it and said nothing.

But the rest of the evening, he watched her differently.

Not as a visitor, but as a variable.

Chapter 23 – Strands of Conflict

Ryan wasn't suspicious by nature. But medicine and Shadow Bay had changed that. He'd learned to read between the lines, listen to what wasn't said, and never ignore the feeling that something didn't add up.

And with Arielle, it wasn't adding up.

Not the notebook.

Not her sudden knowledge of Hemovein.

Not her evasiveness about Spechaven Diagnostics.

She had left Sunday morning with a hug, a bright smile, and a light kiss. But in her hurried departure, she'd forgotten her notebook, and by the time her rental crossed the Lane County line, Ryan was already at his desk with the notebook beside him and a search window open on his laptop.

He wasn't prying, he told himself. He was verifying.

The first hour brought nothing unusual. Spechaven Diagnostics had only a shell LLC listed in Delaware. But it wasn't until he cross-referenced executive names from Spechaven's internal memo that he struck something buried deeper.

Arielle's name was attached, not publicly, but on a PDF shared through a biotech insider archive forum.

T. Everett – Independent Consultant, BiogenEcell PAC Liaison.

He sat back, stunned.

BiogenEcell.

He'd heard of them only once, in a heated ethics lecture during med school. A *"libertarian-progressive hybrid"* PAC, as one professor had called them, "funded by radical biotech investors, quietly supporting legalized stem cell expansion and embryonic manipulation beyond federal thresholds." It operated in legal gray zones, piggybacking on off-shore clinics, and skirted FDA boundaries by channeling R&D through foreign subsidiaries.

Arielle had never mentioned them.

Ryan kept reading.

Several members of BiogenEcell's leadership board had backgrounds in clinical experimentation abroad. Trials that weren't just frowned upon, they were blacklisted by American oversight bodies. One executive had been quietly banned from Johns Hopkins Medical Research Initiative after funneling fetal cell data into a private startup in Singapore.

And Spechaven Diagnostics?

A known shell. Used to siphon anonymized EHR datasets into proprietary software, software flagged for manipulating outcomes and redacting trial anomalies. Including failed stem cell lines.

The hair on the back of Ryan's neck stood up.

He dug deeper.

He found her name again, this time linked to a presentation event in Geneva, hosted by a group called StemCunbound, where emerging "gray zone" biotech firms sought private funding with no regulatory strings. Arielle had been on the panel. She wasn't some detached consultant. She was part of the machine.

He closed the laptop slowly.

His hands felt cold.

That evening, Ryan walked Stix down the gravel trail near the river bend. The dog ran ahead, leaping over driftwood and chasing shadows, oblivious to the weight Ryan now carried.

He couldn't see a future with someone who supported programs that would have endangered patients like Spencer, his donor. Or who might've trafficked in the same data that almost cost him his life.

It wasn't just politics. It was principle and betrayal.

He didn't call Arielle that night. He didn't need to.

Their next conversation, if there was one, wouldn't be over wine and small talk.

It would be about ethics. And silence. And walking away.

When he returned to the house, Stix curled up near the door and dozed off.

Ryan opened Arielle's notebook one last time, flipped to the back, and found a scribbled page labeled: Potential risk: disclosure if R. gets wind of trial history. Tie it to Dalton's research, unknown but possible. Monitor.

He closed the notebook.

And this time, he didn't put it back.

Chapter 24 – Exit Wounds

Ryan waited two days.

Not out of indecision, just out of courtesy. There were things you owed a person when you'd once imagined a future together. Even if that future was now a ghost.

He called her Tuesday night.

Arielle answered on the second ring. Her tone was chipper, oblivious.

"Hey, I was just about to text you. We're in the second round with Vertex, and Hemovein is merging under a new umbrella, a total rebrand. We're…"

"Stop."

The word came out quiet and flat. But it cut through her momentum like a scalpel.

A pause. "Ryan?"

"I know about BiogenEcell and StemCunbound, and Spechaven. And the presentation in Geneva."

There was silence on the line. Not a surprise. Just recalibration.

"I see," she said finally.

"You weren't just consulting. You were embedded. You sat on panels that defended stem cell sourcing methods that aren't just illegal in the U.S., they're unethical by any standard."

"You don't understand how innovation works."

Ryan's jaw clenched. "You're right. I don't understand using fetal tissue to chase grant money. I don't understand falsifying trial results. And I sure as hell don't understand how you could sit next to me, knowing everything I went through with leukemia, and with Spencer, while being tied to companies that use human lives like prototypes."

"You're overreacting," she said, voice now clipped.

"Those companies operate under emerging frameworks. Regulation always lags innovation.

You think the treatments you benefited from came from saints?"

"No," he said. "But they came from *transparency*. That's the difference."

Another pause. When she spoke again, her voice was distant.

"You're not going to report anything, are you?"

Ryan almost laughed. "You think this is about whistleblowing?"

"Isn't it?"

"No. It's about character. And I can't stay with someone whose values stand on a fault line."

He let it sit.

"Goodbye, Arielle."

"Ryan..."

He ended the call.

The next morning, he dropped her notebook off with the rest of her things at the small private parcel center in town. No note. Just her name and address taped to the top.

By the time he got back to the clinic, the morning staff meeting was already in session. Sydney handed him a fresh report on the AI rollout and smiled as if she'd been silently rooting for this shift all along.

"You look lighter," she said.

"I feel like I finally exhaled."

Ryan took his seat at the head of the table and looked around. Shadow Bay wasn't fast-paced. It wasn't powerful or flashy.

But it was real, and after Arielle, that was more than enough.

Part V

Suspicious Minds

Chapter 25 – What the Roots Don't Say

Ryan had never owned a piece of earth before, not really. The lot behind his A-Frame home stretched gently to the tree line, with just enough slope to keep things interesting. He walked it most mornings with Stix, planning imaginary garden beds and raised planters in his head.

On Friday, he brought it up to Sydney over coffee in the clinic break room.

"I was thinking of putting in a garden," he said casually, flipping through EHR updates.

"A few vegetables. Some herbs. Maybe flowers along the fence line."

Sydney glanced up from her chart notes. "What kind of flowers?"

"I don't know. I admire your flowers and bushes. That pink-petaled bush you have looks pretty hearty. Might be a good starter as I am better with blood than I am with plants."

Sydney froze for just a beat. "The one with long, skinny leaves? Starburst-style petals?"

"Yeah. I think so."

Sydney set her pen down. "That's *oleander*, Ryan. Pretty, but deadly. One leaf can kill a dog or a child."

Ryan blinked. "Seriously?"

"Seriously," she said, trying to sound casual, but something had shifted behind her eyes. "Don't plant it. Especially with Stix around. He digs, remember?"

He nodded slowly. "Good point."

But the way she said it stuck with him. It wasn't the warning. It was the *weight* behind it. Like the plant carried more than just poison in its roots.

"Where did you get your plant?"

"You don't remember, but when I became a Registered Nurse Practitioner, Bill gave it to me as a gift. I never really liked it once I found out it was dangerous. But it is pretty. I probably should get rid of it now with Stix around."

Sydney sipped her coffee, knowing the wind carried no secrets, only the scent of oleander.

Meanwhile, Sheriff Truman had quietly returned to the vineyard, not for formal questioning, but for 'follow-up' interviews with the remaining crew. He asked simple things. Who Cesar last spoke to. Whether Luisa left anything behind. If anyone remembered the make of Cesar's truck. He kept it friendly.

But he was watching Bill.

Bill, for his part, was watching the vineyard.

The place had been operating at half speed since Cesar and Luisa disappeared. He'd hired two part-time workers to keep the vines healthy, but the rhythm had changed. The quiet was too quiet. And Valerie, Valerie was deteriorating.

Migraines, Dizzy spells, and nausea. Her prescriptions weren't working, and when Bill asked her what she last ate or drank before her worst episode, she mentioned a salad with wine from the same cooler where Cesar once kept his lunch.

Something in his gut churned.

He didn't voice it, not yet.

But he found himself double-checking the clinic's stock of cardiac antidotes, just in case.

That night, Ryan sat on his back porch with Stix and a gardening book open on his lap, but unread. His thoughts circled.

The oleander plant.

Sydney's strange expression.

Raincrest Cellars had vines in bloom and secrets buried in the soil.

The clinic had new walls and upgraded software.

But the truth?

The truth was surfacing in slow, patient waves, and Ryan was finally close enough to feel it's undertow.

Chapter 26 – Echoes in the Code

Ryan hadn't planned to spend the entire Thursday morning digging through historical tox screens, but *VitalMind* had flagged a metabolic irregularity in a new vineyard hire. It was supposed to be a one-click review.

Instead, it became a thread he couldn't stop pulling.

The AI suite's retroactive feature had been designed to map subtle medical patterns across time, now tuned to sweep past toxicology reports for cardiac anomalies. Ryan widened the parameters, partly out of curiosity, partly instinct.

Then he found it.

Patient: John Collins. Date of Death: June 18, 2023.
Toxicology Marker: Trace Oleandrin.
Flagged: Not Elevated. Acute myocardial infarction secondary due to chronic alcohol and drug abuse
VitalMind Suggestion: Re-review based on pattern matches to known botanical glycoside exposure.

Ryan stared at the screen. His breath slowed.

Oleandrin.

He reran the analysis twice. Same result. The algorithm had matched oleander compounds, deadly and deliberate, against cardiac failure symptoms.

He had always believed John died of a sudden heart attack. The reports said as much. It made sense.

Until now.

Meanwhile, across town, Sheriff Howard Truman sat quietly in his unmarked truck outside Raincrest Cellars, sipping coffee and scanning activity through tinted windows. It wasn't official yet. But he had reason to suspect that something or someone had been buried in more than just paperwork.

Cesar's absence didn't feel like flight. It felt like an erasure.

No exit calls. No sightings. No trail. Just vanished.

And Truman had learned to follow silence more than noise.

A fieldhand had mentioned seeing Bill working the skid steer late one night. Another noted Cesar accepting a bottle of wine from Bill the same day.

He'd logged it all.

But Bill was careful. Smooth. Never direct. Always one step ahead.

Which meant Truman needed to stay two steps quiet.

Back at the clinic, Sydney sat hunched at her desk, pinching the bridge of her nose. Another round of compliance memos. More required documentation codes. More burnout in the guise of care.

"I'm drowning in forms," she muttered, not realizing Ryan had stepped in.

He leaned against the doorframe. "You sound like someone ready for a career change."

She looked up, eyes tired but amused. "Don't tempt me."

"I'm not. Bill mentioned Raincrest could use someone who knows how to manage people and headaches. Valerie's getting better, but still can't keep up."

Sydney raised an eyebrow. "Wine over medicine?"

"Peace over bureaucracy," Ryan countered. "You've earned that."

She chuckled but didn't dismiss the thought. "John always used to say the paperwork would kill me before the job did."

Ryan swallowed hard. The name hit differently now.

He nodded, smiled gently, and changed the subject.

That evening, Sydney hosted Taco Thursday, a comfort ritual Ryan and Bill had come to depend on. Valerie was laughing again, and Bill had brought two bottles of a test blend for them to try. The air felt light, normal.

The aromas of tacos filled Sydney's cozy log home as laughter drifted easily between the kitchen and the dining table. Bill, expertly assembling another round of tacos, glanced at Valerie, sensing the unspoken cue. Valerie caught his eye and smiled, gently shifting the conversation toward Sydney's recent frustrations.

"Ryan mentioned you've been bogged down lately," Valerie began softly, pouring another glass of the test blend.

"All the paperwork and compliance nonsense taking up your time, leaving less for what you truly love, patient care."

Sydney sighed, nodding as she passed the salsa to Ryan. "It's true. Feels like I spend more hours documenting than actually healing. It's wearing thin."

Bill set down the serving platter and wiped his hands on a kitchen towel, his expression earnest yet comforting.

"We've been thinking, Syd. Raincrest Cellars is turning a promising corner. Solid sales, a good team, and plenty of room to grow. Maybe it's time you seriously considered stepping away from all that bureaucratic hassle. Join us. You could help Valerie, and honestly, we could use someone with your skills and heart."

Valerie reached over and lightly squeezed Sydney's hand. "No pressure, but just think about it. It might be exactly the change you're looking for."

As Ryan dipped a chip in the salsa, something tugged at his attention.

Stix was missing.

He scanned the room, no panting underfoot, no thud of a tail against the cabinets.

Ryan slipped into the hallway, then toward the front sitting room.

There, tucked behind the vintage secretary desk Sydney had kept since before John died, Stix crouched low, ears back, gnawing gently on the carved leg.

"Hey," Ryan whispered, crouching.

"What are you doing?"

He gently pulled the dog back, careful not to draw attention. That's when he saw it, a drawer, slightly ajar, like the chewing had jostled it loose.

He tugged it open and reached behind, his fingers brushing on something firm.

A leather-bound journal.

No label, no locking clasp, just a typical journal.

He opened it carefully, keeping an ear out for movement from the kitchen. Only laughter and the sound of wine glasses being poured.

He read from the journal what Sydney had penned:

John had been a good man before his traumatic brain injury and before he started with his infidelity, drug, and alcohol abuse. It might have all stemmed from his low sperm count diagnosis.

In a moment of selfishness, I confided in the wrong person, your father, Bill, who had experienced infidelity himself.

I never meant for any of this to actually happen, John. When I said I wished you would disappear once I found out about your infidelity, I never dreamed it could become real. It was your father, Bill, who advised me on your continued infidelity relationship with Lynda. Of course, Bill knew my love for gardening, so it was his dangerous idea that he provided me with the perfect antidote, the oleander plant.

Bill, with his charming smile and dangerous idea, had suggested the unthinkable. When John is in a drunken or drugged stupor, just prune a few small pieces of the oleander plant into his iced tea. Trust me, John doesn't deserve you and Ryan anymore.

Every day, I wake up hoping this will be the day the guilt leaves me. But it clings to me, a constant reminder of what I've done.

Ryan's pulse tightened. He flipped the page.

His hands became cold.

His mother had killed John with Bill's help.

Not out of rage.

But choice.

He closed the journal quietly. Slid it back into the drawer and closed it, as best he could. Stix sat beside him now, tail still.

Back in the kitchen, the story rolled on, unaware.

But for Ryan, something irreversible had just begun.

Chapter 27 – Terms of Departure

The conference room at the clinic smelled of fresh coffee and fluorescent lighting. Sydney sat at the head of the table, legal pad in front of her, though she hadn't written a single word. Ryan sat to her right. Across from them, Dr. Bell and Marla from operations thumbed through printed proposals while the new candidate, the knee surgeon, introduced himself with a polished, confident tone.

"Dr. Richard Bennett," he said, extending a hand across the table. "Board-certified in orthopedic surgery. Specialty in knees. Oregon-born, Mayo trained."

Ryan nodded, professional but measured. "You've been practicing in Bend?"

"Until last month. I'm ready for a shift back to small-town medicine. Shadow Bay's numbers support it: high demand, aging joints, and enough weekend athletes to keep a table busy."

Dr. Bell leaned back. "We've needed someone like you for a while."

Ryan cleared his throat. "Especially with the clinic expanding and Sydney considering... stepping away."

That was the first time it had been said aloud.

Sydney glanced at him but said nothing.

Dr. Bennett turned to her. "May I ask what's drawing you out?"

She smiled politely. "Let's just say it's time for a different pace."

Ryan added, "It would also open up a clean path for Dr. Bennett to step in, not just as a staff physician, but as a partner."

Bell agreed. "We've run the projections. There's margin for it. If Sydney's shares become available, the board will need to vote, but the math makes sense."

Sydney nodded, still noncommittal.

But her mind was already down the hill at Raincrest.

That afternoon, she drove out to the vineyard to meet Bill and Valerie. They were in the main office; Valerie was sorting invoices, and Bill was marking barrels for reserve bottling.

"I need to ask you two something," Sydney said, bypassing pleasantries.

Bill looked up. Valerie raised an eyebrow.

"Are you serious about me joining you? As a partner, not just a helping hand?"

Bill leaned back in the leather armchair near the tasting room fireplace, the late afternoon light catching the ruby glow of the Pinot Noir in his glass.

"You know," Bill said, swirling his wine with practiced ease, "I think we've finally turned the corner here at Raincrest."

Sydney raised an eyebrow, intrigued. "Turned how?"

"It's subtle," he admitted. "But the kind of subtle that matters. Our direct-to-consumer sales? Up by twenty percent over the last quarter. Online orders are steady and climbing now, not just one-offs, but repeat buyers. The new email campaign's pulling its weight, and the subscriber list grew faster last month than it has in six."

"That's promising," she said, leaning forward.

"More than that," Bill continued. "Our customer acquisition cost is down. We're pulling in new buyers without burning through marketing dollars. Valerie, with a little marketing help, has cleaned up our online storefront. It turns out a micro-influencer from Portland posted a reel about our limited reserve. It caught fire. We had to start turning down event tastings just to keep up with inventory."

Sydney smiled, impressed. "So, people are noticing."

"They're not just noticing," Bill said, eyes lighting with quiet confidence. "They're talking. We've had three different bloggers call us 'the next boutique breakthrough in the Valley.' Wine & Corks gave us a spread, and a Seattle sommelier mentioned us in a podcast last week. That kind of organic buzz? You can't buy it."

He sipped and nodded at the Pinot Noir in his glass. "The crazy part is, we're finally getting away with charging what this bottle's actually worth. The brand is getting stronger. Perception, influence, loyalty. It's all shifting. People aren't just buying wine. They're buying the Raincrest story."

Sydney looked out over the hills, her gaze following the rows of vines as they dipped and rose like the rhythm of a well-lived life. Bill wasn't just making wine; he was building something solid.

"And you're saying there's room for me in that story?" she asked quietly.

Bill smiled. "You're not the only one burned out by policy and paperwork."

Valerie gave a tired nod. "I love this place, but I can't do it alone anymore. Not at the level we're aiming for."

Sydney crossed her arms. "Then show me the books. ROI, supplier chain, the risk assessment. If

I walk away from the clinic, I'm not looking to volunteer, I'm looking to reinvest."

Bill stepped to a cabinet and pulled out a leather binder. "It's all here. Margin projections, distribution channels, even an offer from a Portland wine shop that wants a private-label deal."

Valerie added, "We'd match your clinic income within eighteen months, maybe faster with your name in the mix."

Sydney flipped through the binder. It was tighter than she expected. Bill had done wonders in a short period here. The projections were almost too clean.

"You're both sure?"

Bill gave a knowing smile. "The only question is, are you?"

That evening, back at her home, Sydney reviewed the buyout clauses in her clinic partnership agreement. The terms were reasonable. Her shares would transfer with board approval, likely to Dr. Bennett, if the vote passed. Her name would come off the signage within six months.

It felt surreal. But also… inevitable.

Meanwhile, Ryan stopped by after a late clinic shift and found her in the living room, binder and clinic documents spread across the coffee table.

"You're going through with it?" he asked.

"I think so."

He sat down slowly. "Did you talk to Bill and Valerie?"

She nodded.

There was a pause. Something unspoken lingered.

Then Ryan said, "You sure about Bill?"

Sydney looked up sharply.

Ryan's expression didn't change, but his tone had.

"Why do you ask?"

He shook his head. "No reason. Just... he's involved in a lot these days."

Sydney didn't press, but her instincts tightened.

Somewhere between the clinic and the vineyard, something had shifted in Ryan's voice.

He wasn't just her son anymore. He was a man sorting through a truth she hadn't planned on him knowing.

Chapter 28– Circling Shadows

The vineyard was still, dew clinging to the trellis wires as Bill walked the lower rows with a mug of black coffee. The stillness didn't calm him like it used to. It felt watchful. Measured.

Footsteps on gravel broke the quiet, Ryan, arriving earlier than expected, with Stix trailing a few steps behind.

Bill waited.

"Morning," Ryan said without a smile or preamble.

"You're early."

Ryan fell into step beside him. "Been reviewing some old records at the clinic."

Bill said nothing.

"*VitalMind* flagged a couple of things. Unusual toxicity markers. Nothing in the new charts. Just older reports."

Bill kept walking. "Meaning?"

"Meaning I ran a deeper scan on two names: John Collins... and Mark Cavanaugh."

The name hung in the air.

Ryan didn't elaborate. He didn't need to.

Bill stopped at the edge of a drainage ditch and looked out over the eastern slope.

"Some things don't show up on a screen," he said.

"No," Ryan replied. "But they show up when someone builds a pattern from the right angle."

Bill met his eyes. "You got that angle yet?"

"Not all of it. Just enough to make me ask questions."

Bill nodded, a gesture as casual as it was calculated. "Questions are fine. Just don't go building answers too early. They'll box you in."

Ryan turned to go. "Appreciate the advice."

Bill watched him disappear up the path, then reached into his back pocket, pulled out a small notebook, and jotted a few words:

"Ryan digging – early but focused. Adjust timelines."

Then he turned back toward the rows.

At the sheriff's office, Howard Truman sat in front of his aging desktop, scrolling through county mapping requests. A new request had just come through from his input: satellite overlays of Raincrest Cellars, current season and last.

He had also reached out to an agricultural engineer on contract with the state, asking whether undocumented trenching or soil disturbance could be picked up via elevation heatmaps.

On a separate notepad, he'd written two names:

Cesar

Luisa

He boxed them off and underlined the word: "discrepancies."

Bill hadn't slipped yet.

But Truman was close enough to hear the gravel shift under his boots.

Sydney stood in her kitchen, an open bottle of Raincrest Pinot on the counter, and the partnership buyout agreement spread across the table. Her name was neatly typed at the bottom. A signature line waited patiently beside it.

She stared at it for a long moment.

Then signed.

No hesitation.

The paper curled slightly as the ink dried.

The phone rang, it was Valerie. Bill had dropped off the profit-sharing ledger and included an updated projection showing Sydney's initial ROI if she came on in time for pre-holiday distribution.

Sydney smiled faintly. She was ready.

But before she could respond, her eyes drifted to the secretary desk in the front room.

The bottom drawer sat askew, slightly ajar. Silent. Too silent.

And somewhere in the walls of that silence, she felt Ryan's eyes watching, not accusing, but seeing more than he had before.

Chapter 29 – A Release

Sydney had always imagined that walking away from medicine would feel like failure.

But as she stood in the clinic's break room, surrounded by polite smiles and a sheet cake with her name piped in fading buttercream, she didn't feel failure. She felt a release.

Dr. Bell offered a brief and respectful toast.

"Sydney's steadied this ship through every storm we've faced. She's earned her next chapter."

Applause followed. Hugs. A few well-meaning jokes about wine and early retirement. Ryan stood near the doorway, clapping softly, unreadable.

She met his eyes only once. He held her gaze just long enough to say nothing.

Sydney signed the final buyout paperwork that afternoon. Her shares were transferred to the clinic, soon to be offered to Dr. Bennett. The staff would carry on, and the patients would be cared for.

And she would be done.

Bill was waiting at Raincrest with two sets of books, a fresh invoice draft, and a checklist that looked more like a campaign strategy than a vineyard plan.

Valerie met her at the edge of the crush pad and pulled her into a hug. "You're going to do great here. I'm so glad you're coming aboard."

Sydney took in the rows of grapes, the hum of activity, and the smell of wet soil and fermenting fruit.

It felt like anything but medicine.

Bill handed her a folder. "Partnership terms. Don't worry, no surprise clauses. You're an equal from day one."

Sydney opened the folder and scanned it. ROI projections. Equipment investments. Marketing initiatives. Local vendor ties. It was all there, tight, lean, and promising.

But she noticed something else. The supplier list included companies she hadn't seen before, names with no physical address. Just routing numbers.

She made a mental note. Nothing to flag yet. Just something to watch.

"Congratulations," Bill said.

"Let me show you the operations shed. We've cleared out the old office and gave you the side with the best view."

They walked, and for a while, it felt like hope.

Until Bill said, offhandedly, "I saw Ryan the other morning. He's got questions."

Sydney slowed slightly. "About?"

Bill gave a faint shrug. "The past. The vineyard. The usual things people dig into when they're not sure what they've found."

Sydney didn't reply.

Not yet.

That evening, Ryan drove past Raincrest but didn't turn in. He kept going, eyes on the vineyard. On the slope. On the disturbed soil near the old irrigation line.

He pulled over at a turnout and shut off the engine.

He thought about John's report. About Mark's flagged death certificate and lab report. About the scent of oleander blooming just outside his mother's kitchen window.

There was no hate, not for Bill, not for Sydney.

But he couldn't unknow what he now carried.

He turned the engine back on and drove home, Stix pressing his nose to the side window.

Back at Raincrest, Sydney stood alone in her new office as the sun dipped over the vine rows, casting long shadows across the ledger open on her desk.

She felt the air shift. The weight of her decision. The subtle pulse of something still buried but not forgotten.

Behind her, the vines rustled.

Out in the dark, the past was unsettled.

Chapter 30 – Depth and Distance

Sheriff Howard Truman stood at the edge of the south slope of Raincrest Cellars, just past the lowest vine block, clipboard resting lightly in his hand.

He wasn't taking notes. He was listening.

The wind rustled dry leaves across a surface that was just a little too smooth, a little too level for a hillside that had once been rougher terrain. It wasn't natural. It was engineered, filled in, and tamped down.

He crouched and examined the soil.

It wasn't fresh. But it wasn't old either. And it matched a spot he'd flagged from a drone scan two weeks earlier.

It was time to stop circling.

He opened his phone and typed a short message to the county environmental officer:

"Request expedited variance – soil compaction inspection, Raincrest Cellars, southeast block. Unofficial."

He closed his phone and looked uphill toward the barn and tasting room.

Bill had been quiet lately.

But Truman had learned long ago that the quiet ones were always writing the most dangerous stories.

Ryan stood alone in the lab, staring at the blood typing kit and the original report he'd run quietly two weeks ago.

Type A+.

It matched Mark Cavanaugh's chart from three years ago, when the former vineyard owner had been treated at the clinic for a work injury.

The blood sample had come from Bill, off-hand, casually, with just the two of them in the know.

"Found something odd on an old pair of pruning shears in the shed. Mind running it?" he'd said.

Ryan didn't think much of it at the time.

But now?

VitalMind had pulled archived health records and incident logs and flagged an inconsistency: the coroner's summary for Mark's death listed *"blunt force trauma consistent with a fall,"* but no one had tested the wound geometry against the tool Ryan now suspected had delivered it.

And Cesar? Gone. Vanished.

No records. No exit.

Just one undocumented migrant worker with a growing temper and a history of confronting Mark over low wages and "respect," according to notes in Valerie's early employee logs.

The pieces were no longer scattered. They were forming a picture.

And the man who had handed him the blood sample, the man who raised him when John couldn't, had been the one tying the bow on every loose end.

Bill stood in the bottling room, watching pallets being stacked for next week's shipment. Valerie called out something from the office about a miscount, but Bill didn't respond right away.

He was thinking about Ryan.

The boy had been asking different kinds of questions lately, direct, but loaded.

And Bill had learned how to read when curiosity turned into suspicion.

That was the problem with doing the necessary thing: eventually, someone decides to put it under a microscope.

And Ryan, like Truman, was getting closer to the edge of the truth.

He pulled out his phone, updated a note under "Crisis Timeline."

"If Truman pushes, shift narrative to Cesar as aggressor – self-defense claim?
Ryan may need a distraction. Consider redirection."

He locked the phone and stepped out into the vineyard with a rake in one hand and something far heavier in the other.

Chapter 31 – The Line Beneath

Sheriff Truman stood alone on the lower slope of Raincrest Cellars, boots pressed into the crisp edges of the south block, prime Pinot Noir territory. The vines curved in quiet rows behind him, but he had no interest in grapes.

His eyes were on the ground.

The soil was wrong here. Leveled. Packed. A faint discoloration around the edges told him someone had tried too hard to make it blend. It wasn't erosion, it was concealment.

Truman crouched and took a photograph with his phone. The search variance tucked in his jacket was valid now, approved under environmental grounds. But he hadn't executed it yet.

He wanted one more look. One more read of the land before he acted.

And the land was talking.

Ryan sat alone at the clinic, *VitalMind* pulled up on his office tablet. He toggled between data points: the blood sample from Bill, Mark Cavanaugh's old medical records, and the pruning tool that matched Mark's fatal injury wasn't in the original investigation.

The blood sample, verified as *Type A+*, lined up with Mark's 2019 chart after a work accident.

The math was simple.

Cesar killed Mark.
Bill cleaned it up.
And Cesar... vanished.

But the story hadn't ended there.

Now, Ryan had to decide if he wanted to finish it or become part of the cover.

Bill moved methodically through the operations shed, checking the month-end shipment tallies for the Pinot Noir barrels. Chardonnay had been lighter this season, but their Pinot yields were strong, justifying the private label deal he'd negotiated with the boutique distributor in Portland.

He glanced out the window and spotted the sheriff's cruiser parked at the bottom of the hill.

Truman was walking the perimeter again.

Bill smiled faintly, not out of pleasure, but calculation.

He'd expected this.

He had already adjusted the terrain near the trench. Sprinkled vine trimmings. Deep-watered the rows to soften any signs of digging and skid steer work. Buried old rebar to muddy ground-penetrating radar. He even had a falsified soil amendment record backdated and logged with the vineyard's agronomist.

The man wanted to dig. Let him dig.

Bill would be waiting with paperwork in hand, and nothing but Pinot vines to show for it.

Sydney wandered the upper Chardonnay block that afternoon, clipboard in hand, scribbling a few pest monitoring notes. She was still adjusting to vineyard work, but something about the rhythm of the place grounded her.

Cesar and Luisa had come up in conversation a few times, in passing. A migrant couple, threatened by ICE. Then suddenly gone.

Valerie chalked it up to nerves and stress, with rumors about ICE checks at other vineyards. Sydney hadn't pressed. She didn't know them.

Not really. She assumed they'd moved on.

But occasionally, when she passed the rows down by the irrigation line, she caught herself pausing, like something unseen was pulling at the edge of her thoughts.

She shook it off. The grapes didn't ask questions.

That evening, as twilight crept over Raincrest, Sheriff Truman stood at the edge of the irrigation trench, search variance in hand. The ground still looked too even, too perfect.

He looked up toward the house.

In the upstairs window, Bill stood watching, motionless, his face half-lit by amber light.

They held the gaze a few seconds too long.

Then Truman turned, walked back to his truck, and drove off into the dusk, without a word.

Bill watched until the taillights disappeared behind the Chardonnay block.

Then he reached for a bottle of their 2022 vintage.

He poured one glass and toasted, quietly, to timing.

Ryan sat on his back deck that evening, watching Stix tear into the dry leaves piling in the yard.

He hadn't told Sydney what he knew.

He hadn't told Truman what he suspected.

But in his gut, he felt it.

Mark hadn't fallen.

Cesar hadn't fled.

And Bill hadn't hesitated.

Part VI

The Burden of Guilt

Chapter 32 – Tilt

Sheriff Truman stared at the satellite map stretched across his desk, marked with red notations and drone timestamps. The southern irrigation trench at Raincrest Cellars was still sitting in the back of his mind like an unanswered question.

His search hadn't turned up anything definitive. Bill Collins had been too prepared, too clean. The soil had been amended. The paperwork was precise. And the environmental records were backdated with plausible signatures.

But Howard wasn't done.

He just knew when to step back before tipping his hand.

Ryan sat in his small kitchen, *VitalMind* open, sifting through the raw metadata he hadn't shown anyone. The blood sample Bill had casually dropped off weeks ago still ran through his mind; it was a match to Mark Cavanaugh's A+ blood type.

He thought of the pruning hook. The angle of trauma. The quiet note in the medical log from Mark's previous injury in 2019.

Then he thought about the journal, Sydney's journal, tucked back inside the damaged secretary drawer where Stix had uncovered.

She had written about John and how she had used oleander to shield Ryan.

But Ryan had grown up believing John died of heart failure.

There had never been an autopsy. Just a quiet cremation. A quick, convenient end.

The plant, the pink oleander, still bloomed at the edge of his mother's garden. A plant Bill had given her, likely knowing exactly what it was. Bill's wife died suddenly as well, heart failure...

Ryan stared through the window. Stix lay sprawled in the yard, twitching in sleep, the only innocent one in all of this.

Raincrest Cellars had two secrets buried beneath its vines: Mark hadn't fallen, and Cesar had never left.

Back at Raincrest, Bill made his rounds through the Pinot Noir rows, noting stress patterns near the wire trellising and checking the late-season clusters.

The harvest would be strong this year.

He paused at the edge of the south trench, where a line of vines looked perfectly normal to anyone else. But not to him. He knew what lay beneath.

Cesar had killed Mark. That much was true.

But the moment Bill had realized there would never be a trial, never be justice, not with Cesar's undocumented status, not with Valerie's migraines and disarray, he'd made a decision.

Handle it. Quietly. Permanently.

And now Ryan was circling too close. Sheriff Truman, too.

But Bill had one advantage that neither of them did. He wasn't burdened by doubt.

Sydney walked through the back garden that evening with a mug of tea, absently tracing her fingers along the fence line. The oleander bush had grown wild lately, pink petals clustering in defiant blooms.

She had almost asked Bill to pull it. But she hadn't yet.

She had told Ryan that oleander was dangerous, yet Ryan was suspiciously silent.

She didn't know he'd read the journal. And she didn't realize yet that the secrets between them were now one secret too many.

Chapter 33 – The Weight of the Roots

The sun hung low over the vineyard, casting a soft orange hue across the neatly trellised rows of Pinot Noir. The crush pad was silent, the day's work done. Inside the storage barn, the scent of earth and wine lingered in the air.

Sydney leaned against a tall workbench near the back wall, arms crossed, her boots scuffed with dust. Bill stood beside her, a glass of wine in hand, scanning the day's inventory notes.

The silence between them wasn't awkward, just heavy. Familiar but weighted.

After a moment, Bill broke it. "I saw Truman again. This morning. Parked down near the lower block like he was waiting for something to move."

Sydney looked up, startled. "Again?"

Bill nodded, calm but alert. "Didn't come to the house. Didn't say anything. Just watching."

A gust of wind whistled against the barn door. Sydney pulled her jacket tighter.

"He's patient," Bill continued. "Like he suspects something's off. He's still looking for a crack with the migrants."

Sydney's thoughts drifted elsewhere, for the third time that day. That morning, she'd passed the old secretary desk and noticed the gnawed corner and scratched bottom drawer. Stix, of course. But something else. The drawer was slightly ajar, more than she'd first realized when noticing the damage. At the time, it hadn't seemed unusual, barely catching her attention, but now she saw the difference clearly. She knelt down, slowly drawing it open further. Inside, papers appeared shifted, disturbed somehow.

Then she froze. The journal.

Ryan was silent about the damage. He hadn't said a word. That silence unnerved her thoughts more than any question would have.

She turned back to Bill. "Do you think Valerie knows something?"

Bill looked down at the rim of his glass. "I think she knows enough to give herself a migraine over it. She's always suspected Cesar was involved with Mark's death...but never was up to pursuing it. She never really trusted my explanation that he just walked off. But she didn't want to see what was in front of her. She still doesn't."

Sydney didn't reply. Her thoughts were spiraling about Ryan.

His late nights at the clinic.
The quiet glances.
The clipped conversations.

The AI-powered *VitalMind* he'd helped implement, able to cross-reference historic clinic data, labs, toxicology trends, and outcomes across patient profiles.

She'd caught a glimpse of one of his dashboards at the clinic before her exit, highlighting flagged similarities in cardiac fatalities involving unexplained arrhythmia and gastrointestinal shutdown.

It was only a moment, but she knew what he was looking at.

John. He was looking at John.

Sydney exhaled, suddenly aware that her hand was trembling slightly.

"Bill," she said, slowly, "if Ryan knows… how do you think he'll handle it?"

Bill's expression didn't change. "He's smart. Idealistic. But also, loyal. The kind that bends before he breaks."

"And if he bends too far?" she asked.

Bill looked toward the darkening vines. "Then we tell him the truth. What we did. Why we did it. And what it cost us to live with it."

Sydney didn't speak for a long moment.

In her chest, something squeezed, a mix of maternal guilt, fear, and grief she thought she'd buried.

She finally whispered in a weak, trailing voice, "I just don't want him to hate us."

Bill's voice was quiet. "He won't. Not all at once. But he'll question everything. And that's what we've earned."

Sydney nodded, her eyes glassy with tears seeping down her cheeks. Somewhere out there, Sydney knew Ryan was already asking those questions.

Chapter 34 – The Unveiling

It was Taco Thursday again.

The table was set, the food was warm, and the drinks were poured, but the mood was unmistakably different.

Ryan had been quiet most of dinner, listening more than speaking. Stix sat loyally beneath his chair, occasionally nuzzling a stray tortilla chip toward his paw without drawing attention.

Bill told a story about a stubborn irrigation valve, and Sydney laughed, but even she noticed the stiffness in Ryan's smile. The boy she had raised was still sitting across from her, shoulders strong, jaw squared, but his eyes had gone distant. Analytical.

Finally, when the plates were pushed aside and the last sip of wine was gone, Ryan leaned back in his chair and spoke.

"I've been using the old data sets in *VitalMind.*"

Sydney glanced at Bill.

Ryan didn't blink. "It's good software. Helps track patterns in labs, diagnostics, and cause-of-death discrepancies."

"Sounds powerful," Bill said cautiously.

"It is," Ryan said.

"Especially when it flags similarities between two cases you'd never think to compare, unless you're looking for signs of oleander poisoning."

Silence. The only sound was Stix quietly shifting on the floor.

Ryan looked at Sydney. "John didn't have an autopsy. And I never questioned that. You said it was a heart attack. Cardiac arrest."

"It was," Sydney said softly, but she didn't finish the sentence.

Ryan continued. "And now, I know that oleander mimics arrhythmia, produces the same signature on an EKG. But unless you're looking for it, it's invisible post-mortem."

Still, Sydney said nothing.

Bill watched her carefully.

"And then I noticed," Ryan added, "that Mark Cavanaugh's death was flagged by *VitalMind*, too. Blunt force trauma. Same blood type. And Cesar? Gone. No forwarding address. No report. Just vanished."

Sydney opened her mouth. Then closed it.

Ryan let out a long breath, leaned forward, hands clasped.

"I found your journal, Mom."

Sydney looked away, her fingers tightening around the stem of her empty glass.

"I wasn't looking for it," Ryan continued. "Stix chewed the cabinet. I pulled the drawer open to clean up the mess. And it was there."

Bill's face was unreadable.

"I read enough to know you gave John the oleander," Ryan said.

He paused, then looked at Bill.

"And I know you gave her the oleander plant." Still, Bill didn't flinch. Ryan stared at both of them.

"You buried Cesar."

A statement. Not a question.

Bill exhaled once. "Yes."

Sydney closed her eyes.

Ryan stood and walked toward the window. The sky was dark now, stars scattered in between clouds that hadn't quite decided whether to move in or pass.

"I've spent months looking at data. Searching for truth," he said. "*VitalMind* doesn't have everything; some files are too old or missing completely. Like Grandma's."

He turned toward Bill, just briefly.

"But patterns... they don't always need a full record to point toward a conclusion."

Neither Sydney nor Bill responded.

Ryan's voice softened, but the weight remained.

"The answers were under my own family's roof."

"You were never supposed to carry this," Sydney said quietly.

"But I do," Ryan replied. "Because you raised me to ask hard questions. To find the truth, even when it hurts."

He turned to face them both.

"I can't unsee what I've seen. Or unread what you wrote. But I can also tell you this..."

He looked at Sydney. "You carried me through cancer."

He turned to Bill. "And you taught me how to live like a man."

He hesitated.

"I don't know what I'm supposed to do with this. Not yet. But I know this much: you saved my life. More than once. And whatever else happened... I'm still standing because of you."

Neither Sydney nor Bill moved.

Ryan walked over to Stix, clipped his leash to his collar.

At the door, he stopped and turned back.

"Secrets have a way of pulling roots deep. But I guess the question now is whether we let them grow into something poisonous, or just... prune them and keep moving."

Then he opened the door and was gone.

Chapter 35 – Harvest Moon

The clinic felt quieter now.

Sydney's office had been cleared out; photos boxed, diplomas removed, and the aloe plant she'd nurtured since her first week there was gone from the windowsill. The new orthopedic suite, funded in part by Ryan's inheritance from Dr. Avery, was humming with patients, and the lobby buzzed with steady traffic.

But Ryan noticed something else: the space felt a little lighter. Like whatever weight had lingered had now been... redistributed.

He stood at the reception counter reviewing charts when the front door opened and in walked Dr. Grace Morgan, her crisp white coat bearing the Willamette Sacred Heart emblem.

He recognized her from a recent critical-care consult, an anesthesiologist with steady hands and sharper wit. She had been assigned to cross-train at regional clinics as part of a new collaborative initiative.

"Dr. Bell around?" she asked the nurse, eyes scanning the space.

"She's with a patient. You can check in with Dr. Collins," the nurse replied, nodding toward Ryan.

Ryan stepped forward. "Dr. Morgan. Good to see you again."

She smiled. "Likewise. I heard your mom left the clinic."

He nodded. "She did. Joined Raincrest Cellars vineyard."

Grace laughed. "That sounds... idyllic."

"It has its complications," Ryan said. "But I think it suits her."

He motioned toward the staff lounge. "You've got time for coffee?"

"Sure. If it comes with a side of sarcasm and something sweet," she said, walking beside him.

As they moved down the hallway, a soft moment passed between them, unspoken, but lingering. Something new. Something possible.

That evening, Ryan drove out toward Raincrest.

The vines shimmered in the dusk under the harvest moon; their curled leaves were edged with fire-orange. The air was ripe with the scent of fermentation and woodsmoke, drifting up from a small fire pit near the crush pad.

Bill and Sydney sat at the edge of the fire, nursing glasses of Pinot, Stix curled at Sydney's feet, paw twitching in dreams.

Ryan approached slowly, hands in his jacket pockets. Bill looked up first, then Sydney.

He didn't speak right away. Instead, he sat down, reached for the wine, and poured himself half a glass.

"I think I'm ready to leave it behind," he said.

Neither of them moved.

"The journal. The data. All of it," he added. I've made my peace with knowing."

Sydney reached for his hand, and he let her hold it.

"Just promise me," Ryan said, looking at them both. "No more secrets. If we're going to be a family, it has to be real."

Bill raised his glass. "To what's real."

Sydney smiled faintly. "To what's left after the pruning."

They clinked glasses under the moonlight, letting the fire crackle, the vineyard stretch, and the air finally settle.

In that moment, three imperfect people, bound by love, guilt, and choice, found something rare: a quiet kind of forgiveness.

Not absolution. Not forgetting. Just understanding.

And that, Ryan thought as he glanced at the stars overhead, might be enough.

From Valerie's house, the screen door creaked open, and Valerie's voice floated down the gravel path.

"Dinner's ready! And don't make me call twice, it was Mark's favorite."

Sydney stood first, brushing off her jeans. "She always said that pasta tasted better with Pinot."

Bill chuckled. "That was Mark's theory. I just think she put in a little extra love when she made it for him."

Ryan smiled, finishing the last sip of wine and giving Stix a gentle pat before they made their way toward the house, the porch light casting a soft glow through the pines.

Inside, the table was set for four, steam rising from a bubbling pan of baked rigatoni, its scent rich with garlic and thyme.

They took their seats, no more secrets, no more shadows, just the quiet comfort of food, family, and a second chance.

As the first bite passed, Valerie glanced at them all with a knowing look. "It's good to have a family in my home again."

And for the first time in a long while, it truly felt that way.

After dinner, Sydney, Ryan, and Bill thanked Valerie for the evening's warmth before retreating to the porch of the old tasting room, glasses of wine in hand. The stars hung quietly above them, and the vineyard stretched out in gold-tinged silence.

There was peace, but also gravity in the quiet.

They had weathered storms, both real and buried. Mark was gone. Valerie's land now entwined with Sydney and Bill's venture. Ryan's near engagement had quietly dissolved, undone not by confrontation, but by truths rising too close to the surface. There had been no police inquiries, no arrests, no trials, just a slow, quiet unraveling.

Sydney never told him everything. She never had to. Ryan had stopped asking. And Bill had stopped answering.

"Funny how the land holds everything, isn't it?" Bill said, eyes fixed on the rows of vines, now dim silhouettes against the night.

"It remembers," Sydney replied. "But it doesn't judge."

Ryan nodded, watching shadows bend across the earth.

"We do what we have to. Then we live with it. That's the price."

A long pause followed. The wind stirred through the leaves, a hush that felt like whispered absolution.

Bill lifted his glass. "To choices and to family, whatever the hell that means."

They clinked glasses. Three survivors. Not saints. Each carrying secrets like stones in their pockets, not to be discarded, but carried, understood, endured.

The porch now bathed in quiet light. The vineyard behind them. The harvest moon dipping low, and a silence filled with both what's known... and what's chosen never to be said.

Epilogue – Beneath the Vines

Raincrest Cellars hummed with energy as the fall wine club event kicked off under string lights and a crisp October sky. Sydney was in her element, clipboard in hand, welcoming guests near the barn-turned-tasting room, her smile genuine, her step lighter than it had been in years.

Bill stood off to the side, pouring samples of the new vintage, chatting comfortably with locals and club members about yields and weather patterns. His back was to the vineyard, but his ears remained sharp. Always listening.

Yet, despite the festive air, Bill's gaze repeatedly drifted to the south block, to that one row of vines where the leaves had resisted the season's gold and crimson palette. There, foliage still clung to an odd vitality, richer in hue, slower to turn, almost defiant against the onset of fall. Clusters had been harvested weeks earlier, but that row had seemed denser, more vigorous, even then—a ghost vine phenomenon or *a dead giveaway*. Ryan had casually remarked just a few days before, as he puzzled over the curious soil samples Sydney had shown him.

Ryan himself arrived late to the gathering, Stix trotting dutifully by his side, leash slack. Spotting Dr. Grace Morgan near the Chardonnay table, he waved casually. She returned his greeting with a warm, easy smile, raising her glass slightly in invitation.

As twilight settled, Valerie called out that dinner would soon be served. Aromas of rosemary bread and roasted tomatoes drifted invitingly through the air. Guests began moving leisurely toward the long tables set with rustic elegance.

But out by the edge of the south block, just beyond the irrigation trench where Cesar lay hidden beneath rich Willamette soil, a delivery-type van idled near the fence line. A man in dark jeans and a tan utility jacket stepped from the vehicle, pausing briefly. He checked a faded photograph against the rows of vines stretching toward the event, his expression unreadable but purposeful. His gaze lingered suspiciously long on the thriving ghost vines.

Sheriff Truman watched the stranger quietly from the shadows of the barn. No badge. No vineyard pass. No introduction. Truman remained still, noting every detail.

The man in the jacket scribbled something into a small notepad, his movements deliberate yet cautious. Then, glancing once more at the unnaturally robust grapevines, he moved silently back toward the van, disappearing quickly into the growing darkness.

Early the next morning, a simple folded note appeared on Sheriff Truman's desk, reigniting questions that many had mistakenly thought closed:

South block. Vines too lush. Soil too rich. Secrets beneath?

Truman leaned back in his chair, the cryptic message echoing softly through his mind. He thought again of Bill's carefully neutral expressions, Sydney's composed charm, Ryan's scientific curiosity.

Peace, it seemed, was once more slipping beyond reach. And beneath the thriving vines at Raincrest Cellars, secrets buried in darkness began reaching inexorably toward the light.

A Special Thanks

Lea,

I would like to take a moment to express my gratitude for your unwavering support and understanding as I dedicate time to my writing. Your encouragement has been my anchor, allowing me to pursue a passion that wasn't always there.

Thank you for being my rock, my aging cheerleader, and my inspiration. Your love and belief in me make all the difference. I'm truly blessed to have you riding shotgun.

About the Author

Steve starts each day with an Irish coffee or two, embracing the sunrise and the seasonal changes that come with it. An avid outdoorsman and sportsman, he appreciates the companionship of his wife and a loyal dog by his side. Enjoying a craft beer or a glass of red wine, and a good sports contest are among his favorite pastimes. Living in the beautiful expanse of Northeastern Wyoming, he finds that life is truly best on the road less traveled.